THE
ANCIENT BURDEN
OF MISERY

THE

ANCIENT

BURDEN OF

MISERY

T. C. WALTERS

ISBN : 978-1-7373596-0-9 (paperback)
ISBN: 978-1-7373596-1-6 (eBook)

Published by Cortland House

ACKNOWLEDGEMENTS

A great well-wisher to this book is a gal called Michele Reynolds. She sparks my creativity and breathes warm whispers of delight into this story. She has lived long in San Francisco and has embraced all its joys and delights. Mary Stevens is one more unique lady. She has pushed the button on ideas and grammar in the novel. She also has a tremendous gift for sending A-1 emails that lift my spirit. Her wit and wisdom are awesome. And, finally, the one gangster who has contributed most importantly to my fiction writing: Jerry Cleaver. He's gone to the happy hunting ground now: he died years ago. But when he was walking on this planet he taught, lectured, and wrote about how to write a book. Many people all over the world are grateful that he shared his knowledge and writing excellence.

CHAPTER 1

Matt Hastings had a farm near the small town-like city of Cle Elum. It was in Washington, The Evergreen State, with spectacular views of the Cascade Mountains and lush forests. The winding Yakima river flowed close to Cle Elum, and was outlined by beautiful trees and handsome hills. Matt's farm was dear to his heart and it had been in the family for three generations. His father had taken time throughout the day to love him and hug him while teaching him to not only grow raspberries and blueberries, but how to raise chickens, train horses, herd sheep, and wrangle cattle as well. He had been the greatest father in the world. Matt had cherished all the moments of being with his father. When his dad died while trying to save the horses from a fire, his three uncles took over the job of raising young Matt and building his courage. Eventually Matt gained experience and a loving family of his own.

Right now he was lounging on a long covered porch outside his wooden house. He was looking over toward the old barn next to the house. The barn was built by his grandfather, wide and wonderful. It looked ancient, like a ghost house somewhere in a story book. Different sections of the barn kept needing repair, but it stood the test of time. It was a symbol of dedication and strength. One of his young sons was feeding the horses. The other was banging away boarding up a corner of the barn. Matt loved his life. He wouldn't trade his hard work for a million dollars. The farm, his family, and the spirit of the land were like gifts from God. He was doing his best but the money had always been on the low end, and slow to come in. It was hard being a family farmer surrounded by giant farms. What he needed was—

A deafening explosion came from the back of the barn. Wood scattered in the air. His sons ran to the house.

Matt jumped from the chair as his petite blond wife rushed out from the front door. "Matt! What happened?"

"Go back inside Cindy. Let me find out."

The boys came up the stairs. "Dad. The back of the barn is blown to pieces."

"Tommy, come with me. Billy, go into the house, protect your mother."

Matt and Tommy ran to the back of the barn. The whole wall was demolished. Stacks of hay were scattered over the ground. And all the chickens were dead.

How did this happen? Who did this? Were the boys playing with some ammonium nitrate from the locked cabin? What in hell's name was going on?

"Tommy did you or your brother open the supply cabin?"

"No daddy, no. We didn't touch anything."

Matt and Tommy checked the rest of the barn. Things looked safe. The other walls were intact. He'd call the police and ask for some kind of investigation. The chickens! We needed them. He couldn't afford to buy more.

He started crying. He couldn't lose this farm. His farm was the reason for living, for growing, for trying to become a fire of life, but he was failing. Matt rubbed his wet eyes. Tommy wrapped his arms around his father.

Later that night, they were eating dinner near the fireplace. As always, Cindy cooked the best homemade vegetable beef stew ever, and the buttery sweet cornbread was beyond belief. The kids kept slurping down the stew and gobbling up the cornbread when there was a rather loud knock on the door.

Matt looked at Cindy. She looked back at Matt. He got up from the table and cautiously opened the door.

"Matt Hastings?" a man in some expensive suit asked. Another man, looking sour and stern, was standing beside him.

"Yes."

"You know a Mr. Russell. You're aware he needs your land. He's bought most of the other farms in the area and combined them into one massive property. He's doing this to initiate a large irrigation system for that main farm on the horizon." The man pointed to it. "Mr. Russell has made you several generous offers. You've refused them all. I don't think you want to refuse him again. If you do, your little farm may not survive another explosion. "

"What are you talking about? Were the two of you the ones that exploded my barn?"

"Let's pass on that question. The back of your barn got torched. Period. What's important is, I doubt if you can stand any more trouble. Your future lies with Mr. Russell. Connect with him."

"My future lies with this farm: to be able to grow crops, raise poultry, and graze livestock. At times it's an uphill battle, but my passion never leaves this pasture."

"Nice thoughts Mr. Hastings, but you're a dreamer. Your land is going to be taken from you by force or funds. So your job is to wake up and decide which way you want to go."

This man was insane. Just as insane as that Mr. Russell. If Cindy and the boys weren't here he'd slap them both in the face, throw out four letter words, then slam the door and lock it. "I'll never let go of my farm."

"You're a self-righteous squirt Mr. Hastings. The main question, the only question is: will you accept Mr. Russell's offer, now!"

"I have not accepted it in the past, and I won't now. So why don't you stop your circling? Do I call the cops and get you guys arrested, or are you going to lay down some cash right now for your damage to the barn?"

"Mr. Hastings, think about your farm, and get back to Mr. Russell tomorrow. He'll be expecting your call." The two men turned.

What was going on? He'd given his life for his farm and family. They're intertwined and blessed by God. He wouldn't ever give them up. "Wait. Listen." Matt grabbed one of the men by the shoulder. "You can't come here, dictate an order, and believe I'll follow it. You and your Mr. Russell are totally—"

The second man hit Matt below the stomach. Matt doubled over; Cindy ran over to him.

"Mr. Hastings, call Russell or you'll be in deep-seated trouble." The man pointed toward the fireplace. "And your whole family will be in danger as well." Both men looked around the room, then looked at Cindy who was knelling down next to Matt, and then at the boys who were hugging their parents desperately. With a half-smile on their faces, they left the house.

CHAPTER 2

It was a golden day in Seattle. Elliott Bay was breathtaking, and The Inn at the Pier was shinning like a newborn star.

Gage McClure, the owner of Seattle's only hotel built over the waterfront, and the GM of the hotel, Hiram Smith, were coming down the stairs into the lobby. Their property was called The Inn at the Pier; however, most Seattleites simply called it, The Inn.

"Gage," the GM said, "you were savvy up there in the meeting. Doubt if the Office of the Waterfront will ever question your insight and creativity again. They seem satisfied and content that you'd like to build one more level to the north side of the hotel. Gotta tell you Gage, you're sharp as a sword, and our hotel is too. Hell, you can stop paying me a large salary as long as you'll let me stay in this dream castle forever."

Gage McClure smiled. "You betcha. Even with all the pressures and problems running this hotel, our property is more than a bunch of choice rooms; it's a wonderland of pearly gates, mahogany wood, and mind-blowing views."

"Amen, brother."

They rounded the corner at the end of the stairs and walked toward the large revolving doors. The front desk clerk stopped Mr. McClure. "Sir, there is a message for you." She handed Gage a small envelope.

He opened it and read the note. *I stopped by to see you, but you were in a meeting all morning. Gage, I'm in some trouble and had to see a lawyer. I'll be finished with the man by 2 this afternoon. I'll come by and see if you have time for a talk.*

Matt Hastings

Gage turned back to the girl. "When was he here?"

"About two hours ago."

Gage tightened his lips.

"Something the matter?" Hiram said.

"Not sure. A friend of mine might be in a tight jam." Gage stuffed the note into his pocket and stared angrily at the wall.

Hiram pulled Gage away and walked with him toward a wall of windows. "You want to open up? We're buds. We've clutched confusion more often than a harlot bends her ass on the curbside. What's going on?"

Gage squinted one eye and looked at Hiram. He was the GM of the most exclusive hotel in Seattle, and yet he could talk like a restroom Romeo when he wanted to. Gage slowly shook his head. "Last year Simmons and I took a vacation out in the country and drove along the Yakima River and around Cle Elum. We were on a small gravel road when the car blew a radiator hose. I swerved the car and half landed in a ditch on the side of the road. We were stuck. This was supposed to be a quiet getaway in the fresh country atmosphere."

"What the hell does this have to do with Matt?"

"As the car was hanging in the ditch I was fuming like a fire dog. I was on a road trip to relax, to get away from—all of a sudden there was the sound of horses. I turned. Simmons turned. A man in worn-out overalls came across the road and tied up a team of horses. The man was Matt. He not only offered to drag my car to his barn so he could fix it, but he had his wife meet us at his house. She offered us cranberry cake and coffee on the porch while Matt began repairing the car. In a little over an hour the car was fixed and we started back to Seattle. Before we left, I gave Matt my card and suggested that he and his family should take a short break sometime. I offered him a waterfront suite for the weekend. Why? Obviously, he's a special man, filled with heart and a pack of love."

"Gage, you're unique. Ain't many black belts have a way to attract such an experience. Hell, you attract all sorts of episodes into your life. You're a one-and-only." Hiram slapped him on the shoulder.

"Matt has come to The Inn several times and we've talked about life and the daily grinds of owning your own business. And sometimes we've even talked about fate, like the way Matt and I met, and the way I met you as you were about to slam that owner of a restaurant with your fist in the air."

Hiram cracked a wide smile.

"The last time Matt was here he was getting into some kind of hot water with his farm. Someone was trying to buy his farm against his will. An entrepreneur was developing the area around Matt's farm, and wanted to include Matt's land into the expansion. He was trying to force Matt to sell his farm. The problem seemed to have passed, but now with this note of his I'm not sure what's happening. I'm going to stay here until Matt shows up."

"Good going. I have a meeting with the Getty Group in thirty minutes. I'll be back by 4. You need anything, give a ring." Hiram slapped him on the shoulder and walked away along the wall of windows.

Gage was in his upstairs office. The office was outlined with polished pine and cedar.

Peace of mind streamed through this golden space of grace. From the windows Elliott Bay was sparkling like diamonds. The waves were small but gorgeous. Gage cherished the waterfront, completely and constantly. Besides Simmons, this was his passion for life. His love of life. As he was at his computer, the phone rang. "Mr. McClure there is a Matt

Hastings here at the desk. Should I send him up?"

"By all means."

Vivian Walker, Gage's secretary, escorted Matt into Gage's office.

Gage grabbed Matt's hand and shook it strongly. "Come on let's go out on the terrace."

They sat down as a cool breeze came off the bay. "You don't look too cheery Matt. What's up?"

Matt gripped the arm of the chair a little tighter. "It's becoming a casino economy out there." He waved his hand across the horizon. "Winner takes all. Corporate farmers are trying hard to consolidate the whole damn agriculture industry. As these corporate farmers buy up smaller farms, not only are they able to become more profitable, but they also become eligible for even more federal subsidies—which they can use to buy even more small farms. And get this: among the 'farmers' who get federal subsidies are Bruce Springsteen, Jon Bon Jovi, former President Jimmy Carter, and even Ted Turner. Right now a large farming corporation is trying to take away my family farm with its fields of pleasure and rivers of joy. I'm being pressured to sell, coerced to sell."

"Didn't that lawyer help you today? Can't he?"

"Large scale agribusinesses have the power to manipulate political policy through lobbying and campaign contributions in order to ensure they can maintain large government assistance. No lawyer can stop this is what I found out! I'm out of—" Matt closed his eyes.

Gage got up and pushed his chair away. The water was brilliant blue and the sky was awesome. He gave Matt one hell of a bear hug and turned Matt's chair toward the bay. No doubt about it: the man was definitely under the gun. Sure, he was a small farmer with a lot of determination, but he was being squeezed hard by a company with corruption and cruelty.

Gage shook his head several times. He mirrored Matt in many ways. It was only last year when The Baxter Group almost seized his hotel. Had he been so feeble-minded to never realize his hotel would be the quest of every real estate developer and buyout king?

Had he thought he had the ability to protect his hotel? Had he—all right, all right, knock it off. Remember what Hiram always said: 'Stuff happens, events occur. So what! It's life. Notice your doubts, feel them, but don't judge 'em, and then let 'em go so you can move on to whatever action is best.'

"Matt, let's take a walk on the pier."

As they walked down the terrace stairs and kept looking out to the bay, Matt seemed to have calmed a little of his anxiety. "This corporate farmer is loaded with money and connections. He greased the palm of someone in the WSDA to make a rule that will ban all chickens, goats, and cows from farms in Washington State if there's a residential house less than 250 feet away from the farm animals. There are some residential houses less than that footage around me, so I'm now going to have to get rid of my live stock. It's Big Farm against the Little Farm. Damn it, I need my cows, goats, and my chickens. This corporate farmer is creating ways to force me, and others like me, to accept his bid to buy us out—or—be ruined. He's going to turn our properties into one large farm, stamped with a corporate label. Gage, I'm going to lose my place if I don't find a way to counter this man's offer."

"What's the name of the company, and what's the big-shot's name?"

"Anchor Enterprises. Dillon Russell is the owner."

"Matt, this is all new to me, but there's no way this guy is going to keep pushing you around like this. You're not a grabber, you're a giver. You're very supportive to others, and to your family. I know this. No one is going to take your farm. Look, first we need to gather some info on this Dillon guy. I'm pretty sure I know a man that can help with this. Second: this WSDA—when do you have to comply with their orders?"

"They haven't posted an exact timeline, but it's going to be soon. I'll have to obey or pay some huge fines."

Gage let out a snort. "That is ridiculous. Give me two days to make some contacts and see what information I can get." Gage took Matt's arm. "Matt, we're going to get you out of this hole. And, we'll do it as a tight team."

Matt looked up at the sky, and then over to Gage. "Thank you Gage. I sure needed someone with courage and tenacity. Maybe my life won't be ruined after all. Right now, I've got to get back to my family. They're really nervous about all that's happening; they hate being alone. Please keep me up-to-date on the progress you'll be making, my friend." Matt hugged Gage pretty darn hard.

"What the—" Hiram shouted at Gage. They were in Gage's upstairs office. "You're going to tackle one of the largest money machines in the agricultural business? Do you realize you can damage The Inn? You have no contacts. Will you start thinking straight?"

"I have one connection. I have you."

Hiram looked at Gage with fire in his eyes. "I've never gone into farming. Don't know shit about it."

"But you know a man who has inroads to just about any situation: Tony D'Amato. He helped us out of one jam last year. Can't he try and help us on this one?"

"Gage, he can't keep helping us all the time. And, you're not gonna go out on a limb to help Matt. You have The Inn to think about, and all of us that work here. You need to put all your attention here. Pay attention! Stop your need to be a hero."

"Matt's in trouble. Just like I've been in trouble or you've been in trouble. Hell, you've been thrown in jail for some of your dark clouds. Trouble's part of life. You've said that a million times. We all need help from time to time."

"You're right, I have. But trouble ain't any good reason to go out on a limb and create even more fuck'n trouble. Damn the gods! Gage you need ta—"

"I need to save this guy. Just like I've helped you out of a bag of bricks. And you've sure helped me. You have insight. You get your special vision from two sources: Zen Buddhism and Tony D, who sure ain't no Buddhist, but he does seem to have the gift for doing and delivering. Won't you see if he can find some loopholes into this Dillon Russell? He helped you out of a tight jam, and he helped me out of the mud last year. Can't he help Matt now?"

Hiram started to yell back, but stopped. "This roadhouse is the best in the Northwest. And you're sure no straw boss, you're the best head honcho ever. You don't just talk to me with passion, you talk to our housekeepers, garbage men, and scrub washers with passion. You're unique. OK, I'll go on up to my office, put in a call to Tony, and wait for a return. Meanwhile, why don't you go for a walk, or do some zazen."

"Some what?"

"Zazen, sitting meditation. Damn it, Gage. Cram your ass down on the floor and concentrate on your breathing for five minutes while you toss your thoughts out the door."

CHAPTER 3

The Bank of America Financial Center was the tallest office building in Spokane, Washington, and Dillon Russell had several offices on the 18th floor. Dillon sipped his bourbon and smoked a cigar as he looked out to the downtown. Many beautiful bridges were spanning the river. And there was the majestic Spokane Falls right here in the heart of downtown. He wanted to expand his business offices throughout the whole 18th floor, and with persistence he knew he could. He was after the majority of farm lands here in Spokane County and over in Kittitas County, home to the good ol' city of Cle Elum. A tall dream? Absolutely. But he was gaining leverage on the lands and within the legislature.

Dillon poured some more bourbon and thought about the two counties he loved. Kittitas County grew great grass, alfalfa, and hay. Plus livestock. It brought in over 60 million a year to individual corporate farmers. And, the agriculture industry here in Spokane County generated over $587 million, annually. Dillon smiled to himself. Rich soil, mild temperatures, and enough blasted rainfall made Spokane County one of the top agricultural counties in the United States. Dillon slammed his hand on the desk. He was on the right path. His goals would be reached.

The door to the private office opened and in walked Dillon's son, Aaron. The boy was in his early twenties with a brain similar to his father's. But his heart was moving in a different direction. He was trying to bring peace into himself, into those screwed up mental myths that labeled him inadequate; the myths that had been acquired as he grew up with his father throwing out dashes of disgust. Aaron handed Dillon a manuscript from the WSDA. It was a signed document stating that Matt Hastings had to clear out all his pigs, goats, and cows in one month, because there were residential houses less than 250 feet away from where he kept these animals.

"All right," Dillon shouted. "We've hit the target! This Hastings guy will have to hand over his farm to me or he'll fall apart."

"Not sure this is the right step to take Dad."

Dillon looked up. "What?"

Aaron hated his dad's tone. "This Hastings man has no heavy income, and he has two young kids and a wife he needs to support. The farm was handed down from one generation to the other. He's tied to his land by blood. My bet is he'd let go of part of his land if he could keep enough property to provide for his family. Dad, we get more in subsidies than he gets in a year for working like hell on the farm."

"Aaron, let me ask you, you want to give up your paycheck here and go out and get an ordinary job? The facts of life my boy: Politicians love to talk about the American farmer, but what they usually mean by 'farmers' are giant corporations who donate to their political parties. The American farm policy is in service to corporations like ours, and it's, directly and indirectly, pitted against family farmers. Understand these facts Aaron, or go get a job as a hand packer."

His dad always drew lines in the sand. He needed to be so damn right, so often. "Don't we want to be true capitalists." Aaron knocked off the glass of bourbon on the desk. "And still cultivate that flaky thing you call, compassion! My professor at the university said he encourages employers and employees to not just be diligent in their duties, but also to do a weird thing: smile at each other, and to customers, and to clients. People are important! Aren't they?"

Dillon looked at the bourbon on the floor, and smiled in disgust. "A lofty idea Aaron, but it's only an idle thought. It's not how this company makes over sixty-five million a year. We make our profit with practicality. We push with grit, like they do in Trump Towers, and the JP Morgan group, and the other generators of high income. Are you listening?"

"Of course, grit is important. You can't just smile and be kind while running a company. You have to have aims and brains, too. But isn't kindness a big part of how you should supervise; isn't it a big part of how you should run with the ball in this world? "

"Great! My son's a philosopher. That's good Aaron. But I'm not sure how your slanted outlook will get you the dollars you have right now to buy the BMW you seem to love, the vacations to resorts you admire, and the nightclubs you linger in. This company provides you with a secure life. Do you want to leave the company now and go out and get a 9 to 5 at some gas pump? No, you don't. So shut the hell up, grow up, and start learning the real ropes of life. Right now go and get your report finished. Hand it to me by 3 today."

"Look at you, dad. Do you always have to argue? That's all you do lately. Can't there ever be adjustments? Can't we have talks with compromise?"

"My way provides both of us with opportunities, growth, and luxury. It did for your mother, does for you, and always for me. Now open up to this world of hard guts and big bucks. Get the report done."

Aaron clutched his hands. Would there ever be a way to talk with his dad? Aaron's deep layers of insecurity kept flowing through him. His father always needed to be right. Damn it! He left the room.

CHAPTER 4

Hiram had opened the door to his room on the top floor of The Inn. It wasn't just his office, it was his living quarters too. He cracked open the door of the refrigerator and grabbed a beer. Then he walked to a second bedroom which was his mediation cove. He tore off his pants and sat down on top of a cushion in some clumsy half lotus posture. Sure, he grew up in the slums. Sure, he served time in the joint. Sure, he knew the man Tony D. But blast the night walkers—he didn't want to call up another chit from Tony D. The man already paid him back for the deed he once did. He couldn't keep callin' in more and more favors. Wasn't he sharp enough to take care of any hot water on his own?

Hiram slammed his beer on the floor.

Hold on homeboy, a voice yelled in his head. You gonna go on and cry like a wuss? Or, you gonna help Gage, a man that helped you out of desperation and distress? A man that opened up your courage. You're gonna help him in any way you can. Get it! Now do some fuckin' Buddha breaths and then call the knife-man real gentle like.

After half an hour of deep breathing, Hiram got on the phone and dialed Tony D. The phone kept ringing until a voice got on. "What!" It was a demand more than a question.

"How are you Red?"

A long pause. "Hiram, you're the only man that keeps using that tag. Been a while. I hear that mess with the Baxter group is all washed up. Since you never call about havin' lunch with me, my guess is you're either callin' to tell me you finally got married to a classy broad, or to tell me of another problem with that waterfront chalet which shines in Seattle."

Hiram hated moments like this, when the only thing to do was to suck in air and forget about sounding like a door to door Jehovah asking for some permission to talk. "Red, I'm a bit hesitant but I need to go forward. I need another favor. And no, it ain't about The Inn. It's 'bout helping a friend of Gage's out of a jam. I've always told Gage to reach out and help anyone, just don't go too far. But, as you know, he's got more passion than power when he helps others."

"That's for sure. If he had never bumped into you, you'd be back in the slammer. He reached out, without even knowing you. OK, what's the scoop?"

"It all about corporate farming and corruption. Some mega-buck man wants to take over a section of land in Kittitas, a county in Washington State. The guy, Dillon Russell, has pull and power within the state legislature, and he's going to topple a small-time farmer, Gage's friend. The small farmer is trying to fight back but is losing at every turn. And now the State Agricultural Committee, by being bribed, has issued him a statement that he might lose his property because his farm of crops and cows seems too close to some residential digs. It's bullshit, but it's going to happen unless—"

"Unless someone stops Russell or his corrupt legislators. I'll find out about Dillon Russell. In the meantime why don't you go on over to this Mr. Russell and see if a simple threat can make him ease up. Now get off the phone."

Tony hung up.

The man didn't waste any time with red tape. Never did.

Hiram went back to the cushion and did some deep breathing.

A woman with the face copied right out of Playboy magazine was heading toward The Inn at the Pier. Her skirt was rustling in the wind. Several people turned their heads and looked at her. Simmons Hall kept walking briskly across Alaskan Way and moved onto the pier. As she was reaching the large main doors of the hotel, Gage was saying goodbye to someone. The man got into his car and drove off.

Gage looked up. Simmons kissed him on the lips. "Dear, you're not looking as vibrant as you were in the shower this morning."

He made an effort to smile.

"Come on, let's do what you always get me to do in this gorgeous hotel. Let's go up to your waterfront terrace."

After they sat down on the deck chairs both of them looked out to the bay. Casually Gage touched Simmons' cheek. "I'm the luckiest man alive to have you."

She brushed his cheek. "That makes us twins. I'm the luckiest girl in the world to have you."

He kissed her again. "The man you saw driving away was Matt Hastings. The man—"

"That was Matt you were saying goodbye to? My God, I didn't recognize him. He helped us tremendously."

"That's the main problem. Now, I want to help him. As you know, Matt has a quaint little farm nestled in the woods. It's been passed down from three generations. It's not small, but it's not large. He works his heart to the grind to keep it growing. But a corporation has recently bought out the other farms around Matt, and now wants Matt's farm. Matt can't give it up; he won't give it up. But the head of the corporation is maneuvering like hell. The man has gotten a state agency to pressure Matt into giving up his land. Matt is uptight and edgy. He's tried a couple things to stop this corporation, but none have worked. As a last resort, he came to me for help. Hell, I don't know anything 'bout that business. But damn it, I've got to help him."

"You will find a way."

She could throw out such an easy phrase, but his mind wasn't buying it. And he was beginning to believe he never would! People thought he was some kind of Jesse James: daring and deliberate. But he wasn't. He was often driven by his ringing bells of insecurity: You can't do that; you're not good enough; you'll fail. He constantly had to cover up these mental loudspeakers, and proceed into the blasted unknown. Gage bit his lip. "Simmons, I've talked to Hiram. He's going to contact Tony D and see if we can get any insights into the weakness of this Mr. Russell, the one who's trying to take Matt's farm. In the meantime I've got to find ways to protect Matt. I've got to find some keys that will unlock his problem."

Gage slapped his forehead. "And, blast the ducks, to make matters worse, just yesterday the Houser Group called with a special request. They need to book half the hotel next week. They're sorry for such short notice but they want to strategize on a two-part marketing plan with their subsidiaries, and they really want the calmness of our waterfront. They've always been big business for us, so of course it was approved, but we'll be totally packed. And Marg, head of housekeeping, will be on maternity leave. She's a 24-karat manager. We have plenty of staff but there's no one here with her penchant for precision. Don't get me wrong, I'm glad they're coming, it's just—it's just that I'll need to spend more time here then unwinding Matt's problem. Damn it, I've got pearls of pressure all around me."

"Sweetheart, you've told me one of Hiram's phrases several times: 'You can never put all the pieces together. But you can try to empty your head with wild thoughts, so you can do the impossible, so you're able to go slow, to go fast.' Remember those words. Stay calm. And keep your treasured talents intact. You can do it all."

Gage almost smiled. "My God Simmons, do you memorize all his phrases? Yes, he says that, and I'm trying hard to put it into practice. Hiram's really helping. And, I've relaxed Matt a little. And, you're amazing; you're helping me relax." Gage awkwardly pulled at his shirt collar. "Come on, let's have sex."

She started unbuttoning her blouse.

"Wait! Simmons. Wait! That was a joke."

She bent over and kissed him on the forehead. "I know."

Simmon's took Gage's hand and walked toward the railing. The sky was wild with wonder. The bay was flowing with sparkling waves. "You've got to focus on your efforts to free Matt. Gage, I've been with you over a year. I know what you do to yourself at times. We all have ouches from the past. Take a moment to remember who you really are and what you've really done. You're a well-built, creative entrepreneur. You've got brains, brass, and drive. And . . . you've got me.

They laid down on the patio blanket, and looked out toward the horizon.

CHAPTER 5

Anna Tyers was in the downstairs office looking over the Manager Flash Report. She was new to any hotel management position, but Gage had insisted on having her start training to take over the GM position when Hiram would eventually retire. She was as cute as a girl in a see-through slip, and just as cunning. She'd been a slut as a teen, making bucks with her juice box. She'd been beaten up several times and often thought of the suicide door—until her only friend in the world, Corky, suggested to try and find a job here. Anna smiled, and rolled her eyes a little. Sure, she was wild and adolescent, but Gage could grasp she had the pistol and personality to become a GM.

Hiram strolled into the manager's office.

Anna looked up. "Hey good buddy, where you been?" She loved this man. The guy was gifted with gray matter.

"I'm going over to Spokane to try and convince the dude who's hurting Gage's friend to back off. He's a big business boy. It might help a little if he sees you with me. Most men take second looks at you and smile with a mouth full of wolf whistles. How 'bout you and me hop on a plane tomorrow and talk with the guy?"

"Hiram that's stupid. I'm here to learn about hotel business. I'm here because Gage pays me a good salary, and he trusts me. Stop this bullshit. That friend of Gage's will—"

"Let's see Miss Jazzy, you've been stuck in a mess of problems. Many people get stuck in the hole like you were in. But no one was really reaching out to you. It was Gage, only Gage, that pulled you out of your misery. And yes, he's pulled me out of the mud too. I think Anna, we both need to always be there for Gage. You catchin' my drift?"

"What is it with you? Are you meant to be a Dutch uncle? Always trying to prove that you know what's best? Always trying to prove you're better than the rest of us?"

"I ain't proving nothin'. I'm saying in this hotel, in these digs, everyone has one priority: you help those that work with you. Why? Because everyone in this hotel, every person in the world, has problems. We all need help from time to time."

Anna started to throw back some hot lead at Hiram. Her whole world was spinning around in her head: her shit-ass past, her bucket of bad luck, and her zero chances to be at peace were a constant source of fire. She didn't want to help any fuck'n man with his goddamn problems. Anna started to smack her hand on the desk—but stopped. Without Gage she'd never have gotten onto this new road to begin with. She owed Gage a billion grams of gold for helping her grow. "OK you husky, you make some sense."

As Hiram and Anna were on the flight to Spokane, Hiram leaned back in his seat contemplating the man they were going to see. Tony had called and told him some of the positives and negatives he had dug up about Dillon Russell. Positive: Dillon was sharp as a tack; he was good at masquerading his true intentions. Negative: He had a low boiling point for anger hidden well beneath his mask of brass. Dillon wasn't just an entrepreneur, he was an agitator with brains.

After the plane landed and they were walking down the corridor, Hiram took Anna over to the side wall. "Anna, I think it best your take the next jet back. I was way out of line. You can't help on this. This Dillon character can be a wild card, and he blows bullets with his anger. I have no idea what goes on inside my brain at times. But

I don't want you hurt. Now get out of here and get a return ticket." He handed her some cash.

She threw the bills on the floor and pushed his chest. People stopped and stared at the sexy woman pounding a rugged man.

"Hiram, what are you talking about? You didn't force me to come with you. You made an on-the-front-burner point: We're doing this for the one guy that's helped us both out of a deep well. We owe him, not out of duty, out of love. So button up your heart, pick up the bills, and let's get movin." She kissed his forehead and pulled at his arm as she walked forward.

They hailed a cab and took off for The Bank of America Financial Center, on West Riverside Avenue. They went up to the 18th floor, walked down the hall to an office on the corner, and went in. Hiram asked the receptionist if Mr. Russell was in.

"Yes he is, but he's not available today. There are many programs to attend to."

"I understand," Hiram said, "but I'm sure he'll want to see us." He handed the receptionist a picture of Matt Hastings and a piece of paper. "I think it'll be important to see him."

The woman read the paper. It was a document from the WSDA about the conditions on Matt's farm and the order to get rid of his pigs, goats, and cows. She excused herself.

A minute later Dillon Russell appeared with the document in his hand. "Interesting, Mr. ..."

"Mr. Smith," Hiram said.

"Please come in."

They walked into Dillon's office. Hiram looked around. Hell, the room was like a luxury suite in Gage's hotel. Leather furniture. Persian rugs. Six-piece sofas. Unfortunately, it also had two armed guards. There was also a young boy sitting in the corner.

"I assumed," Dillon said, "this was strictly confidential, only between Matt and the state government. Do you work for the WSDA?" Dillon nodded toward Anna. "Does she?"

"No, she doesn't, and neither do I. You ever heard of TV dinners?"

Dillon tightened his eyes, and frowned a little.

"They're not as gourmet as home cookin'," Hiram said, "but given the right brand, and slap some pesto into 'em, they taste great. Hell, even family farmers use 'em sometimes."

Dillon's face tightened even more.

"Mr. Russell, I'm with no state government. But I know Matt Hastings. He's definitely a family farmer. I know you're trying to grab his land and all the farms around him. Matt ain't no Cadillac man; he's a simple guy honoring his heritage and that old fashioned word called, love."

"Cute Mr. Smith. You speak like a trucker but you're off track and out of line. Why don't you excuse yourself."

Dillon's muscle men started to circle around Hiram.

"You're a corporate farmer with plenty of bank accounts. You make hefty money. That's good. But you got to realize that you're traveling down the wrong road on this venture. You need to—" Hiram quickly turned as he simultaneously pulled out his pocket pistol and kicked the first bodyguard in the balls. He then turned and rapid-fired two shots into the leg of the second bodyguard. He walked over to Dillon and spit into his face. "Mr. Russell, I'm not telling you how to make a million. I'm just saying to leave Matt's farm alone."

"Mr. Smith, who the hell are you?"

Dillon's son jumped up from his seat and dashed over to his father.

"I'm a friend of a friend who knows Matt," Hiram said. "My friend asked me to help Matt out of your pressure box. I understand your motives and your thirst for profits. Just don't mess with Matt any more. The subtraction of Matt's farm from you business strategy surely won't hurt your growth, your EBTs, or any floor trading you're involved in. But if you don't leave Matt alone, you're going to get sparks of fire with some serious trouble."

Mr. Russell hit the intercom and started to speak.

Hiram smashed the intercom box onto the floor.

"You bastard," Dillon yelled. "You can't come in here and pretend you own me. Get out! And yes, I've a well-built agricultural business. It allows people an American dream: to share in the land of this great country. Matt's farm land is getting more and more financially unstable. Do you understand the facts of life, you fucking rogue. His land is decaying, he has no worth to support it. I'm offering money to him so he can retire, and I'll fix his land and have it produce natural food. You're tough, but I suggest you educate yourself a bit more. Now, leave!"

Hiram put his gun back in his coat pocket. "The only education that's needed, is to listen up. You have bucks and brains. That's a given. But you hurt this earth and food products with an overuse of chemicals to support your lands. Right now I don't care about that mess for the moment." Hiram took out a document from his coat. "Just sign this paper saying that you'll stop trying to do anything to takeover Matt's land. Sign it, or prepare for some heavy resistance, Dillon."

"You're a dumbhead. I won't sign any paper."

"Mr. Russell, sharpen up. Corporate farmers live on the doorsteps of legislatures in the state capital. That's a harsh but true fact. You can't keep sustaining your money empire without continuing to corrupt some state official in the WSDA. If you don't sign the paper, I'll find out who the official is, and get both you tossed into a crowbar hotel."

"More threats, Mr. Smith? I don't pay any official. I only do one thing: make money with fierce financial farming. Now if you're through with your shenanigans, exit this office."

Hiram slapped Dillon's face. "I want a copy of your lawyer's name now."

Dillon spit on the floor, and just stared at Hiram. "Go on, abuse me! You'll never get anything out of me. Leave! And take that bitch with you."

Hiram wanted to crack the man apart. Dillon was going to ruin Matt. Hiram snatched Dillon by his shirt and pulled him up and over the desk top. "Mr. Russell, I ain't gonna kill you. But I can try and ruin you. Ever hear of Sterling Administration? They are the biggest support vessel for investors in the US. They deal with stocks and bonds, and banks. They have networks all over the world. I've a close friend who has some good contacts at their headquarters. I'm pretty sure they can find ways to track your money and methods. Then I'll use their info to crash your empire."

"Slick, Hiram." Dillon pulled away from Hiram. "You're definitely a wild boy. But here, in reality land, you're off the mark. Wonder if Matt's farm house got burnt to ashes this week. His barn blown up, and his live stock burned to death. Or wonder if I find ways to crumble Matt's farm tonight? All your intentions will be worthless. All your course and cocky ways will be for nothing. I'll throw this out one last time: get out of my office. "

Hiram closed an eye. "Dillon, you're about to face some fire you've never experienced. The Sterling Administration will unravel you, and I'll find out who you're bribing. You ever spent time in the slammer? Doubt if you'll like it."

Hiram turned, got Anna, and left the office. They took the elevator to the ground floor, and went into a café in the building's mall. Anna looked curiously at Hiram. "All right Hiram, do you think he's going to back off? He sure didn't seem like he would, no matter how gross your threats were."

"As Tony said, he has the guts to be abrupt and smooth at the same time. We'll see which way he reacts to our facts, and then deal with it." Hiram sipped his latte and looked out the window. "It's gettin' pretty gloomy out there. I'll call and see if the plane leaves on time." Hiram opened his cell phone, talked for a minute, then closed the mobile. "We better stay here overnight, the weather is getting tricky. The plane's already delayed. I'll check us in at the hotel here in the mall. Sit tight, I'll be back."

While Anna was thinking how indebted she was to Hiram and to Gage, Dillon's son walked up to the table. "Hello Miss … I'm sorry I forgot your name"

Anna seemed a little startled to see the boy. "Anna Tyers."

"May I sit down?"

She gestured to the empty chair. "Have a seat."

"My name's Aaron Russell. It got a little noisy up there. Your big guy seemed to handle dad's two men pretty well. After you left my father cursed like a windstorm on how they didn't do their jobs." Aaron kept looking at her breasts. "Don't think you won any favors from him. Heck, I don't win much from him either. Can't say I love my dad, but he does take care of the family."

Why's this kid talking like this? Why's he unloading his personal weight?

Aaron looked around the room for a moment. "Sometimes I really don't know what life's about." He held his hands together. "Yeah, my dad knows his direction in life, but I'm not sure he knows the essence of life. He just pushes the money goal in front of me, saying without money you can't buy a future, and you'll run out of fun." Aaron shook his head. "I don't believe that. But, at the same time, I'm not sure really what life is bout. Do you?"

"Well, according to Hiram—the big man that popped your dad's gunmen—life's only real purpose is to end suffering so you can just feel free. We all suffer because we wish something were some way it isn't, or just get dissatisfied with the way things are. Sure, that sounds like it makes sense, but it takes a ton of work, at least for me, to break free of that kind of addiction. Hiram, on the other hand, seems to be able to do just that, to find the light in becoming free. And he tries to help me skip along that precious path."

Aaron blushed a little. "You do have insight Miss Tyers. And resolve. And you're a very pretty lady."

Anna was caught between a question mark and a complement. This boy was obviously nothing like his dad. He was upfront and honest. How did he grow into this quality when his father was a clip artist? "Aaron, how come you know your dad's ways aren't the best? Has your mother influenced this understanding in you?"

"Nope. Mom's been dead for a while. I keep reading a book on Taoism. My dad would never listen to me talk about it. He yells at me to drop this airy-fairy crap and grow up, but it does seem to face reality pretty well, at least for me. I keep reading the book before I go to bed."

"What? Taoism! Good God, Hiram's into Zen, which has a lot of Tao woven into it. This is unreal. Aaron, you're unreal." She bent over the table and kissed his cheek twice. Her breasts were almost sliding out of her spaghetti strap dress.

Aaron's eyes exploded. He blushed like a red flamingo.

Hiram came back to the café. Aaron quickly rubbed his face, trying to erase his colored cheeks so Hiram wouldn't notice them.

"Hiram," Anna said, "you may recognize Aaron here. He's Dillon's son. He was upstairs with all the commotion. He came down here to calm down. He saw me and came over to the table. We've been having some pretty slick talk, far different than anything his dad would shoot the breeze about. And he's getting into Taoism."

Hiram shook Aaron's hand. "When did you start picking up the Tao's wisdom?"

"About a year ago. My family relationships started to get messed up when mom was on the road to dying. Dad got really crazy when mom passed away. He yelled a lot and pushed a lot. One of my friends told me about Taoism, said it would help me flow with the bangs in life. I hear you're involved in Zen. For a tugboat guy you sure don't look very Taoist."

"Actually, Zen isn't strictly Taoism," Hiram said. "Good ol' Buddhism traveled from India to China, and mingled with China's Taoism which brought the deep discipline of Buddhism into ordinary daily life and became Zen, an entirely new school of Buddhism. It then flowed to Vietnam, Korea, and Japan, and started spreading all over the world into old tugboats like myself."

Aaron started to smile. He didn't seem to be carrying the tight baggage he had upstairs with his dad.

"Aaron, I'm glad you're OK. It was tense up there. All I'm trying to do is protect a man and his ranch. One more piece of the puzzle for you boy: life's an adventure if you use your heart and not your head." He gave Aaron a pat on the shoulder, and turned back to Anna. "Anna, come on, we're checked in. We've got some planning to do. Afterwards, I'm going to take a long hot shower."

Anna gave Aaron a kiss. She smiled and left the table with Hiram, leaving Aaron all alone with another red face.

CHAPTER 6

Hiram and Anna had arrived back in Seattle the next day. When the taxi dropped them off at The Inn, they went up to Gage's suite and told him what the hell happened with their talk with Dillon.

Gage slapped the desk. "It seems to me, Dillon may not stop his danger to Matt. But like you said, we'll wait a day and see how he responds to your actions. Right now, let's go down to the dining room and get some topflight food, but give me just a minute, I need to finish a document."

The Inn's kitchen was in full swing. The two chefs were working by the stoves like they were popcorn popping in the air. The waiters were rushing in and out of the swinging doors. Cocktail waitresses were flowing along the dining room floor when—fire erupted from the banquet room!

People jumped from their chairs and ran from the banquet room in fear and panic. Guests in the main dining area also dashed out of the room.

The maître d' called the front desk. Front desk called Gage. "Gage, there's a disaster down in the dining room. And fire is blazing all over the banquet floor. The guests are running wild."

"What the—OK, OK, call the fire department, quickly. And call our maintenance guy, Stevens, on his mobile. Have him come back to the hotel, and have him call his crew back too. We need them."

"Come on Hiram, there's fire in the dining room."

They ran out the door and flew down the stairs. Anna sprinted behind them.

Guests were scurrying wildly through the lobby. Phones were ringing. The smell of smoke was everywhere.

Hiram checked with the front desk. Gage bolted past the main doors and into the banquet room. "Raphael, what's happening?"

"No idea. Everything was going smoothly and then—a blast! A small section of the flooring erupted with flames. Guest's dropped their silverware. Then another small section erupted, and another."

Gage looked around the room. It was almost encircled with small flames. He started to speak when the firefighters came crashing into the room with all sorts of equipment and hoses. The head of the crew told any remaining staff people to leave. When the dining rooms and kitchen were vacant several firemen turned on the extinguishers; others started digging and hacking with axes into the floor.

Guests were arguing with several desk clerks, and Hiram was trying to quiet another group of guests in the lobby. Gage walked behind the desk as an elderly lady yelled at him. "My dinner is gone. I want it back. Bring me food or I will call the owner!"

"Madam," Gage said, "things are pretty confusing right now. The main thing is that you are safe. We will—"

"Safe! I don't want to be safe. I want food."

"Madam, as soon as the fire is out and the kitchen is—"

"Oh screw you. Check me out. I'm going to my room, pack up, and leave." She turned and went to the elevators.

She was not alone, other guests were also leaving the hotel. The front desk was trying hard to calm the crowd. Precautions were being taken, names registered, and assurances were made that the situation would be taken care of professionally and skillfully. Some people listened, other just turned away.

The captain of the firefighters finally came over to Gage. "Mr. McClure, most of the fire is under control. We're going to send a team underneath the pier at the section of your dining area and kitchen. We're not sure how the fire started. We need to do a thorough inspection."

"How long will it take?" Gage asked.

"Can't be certain. We'll check for residue of synthetic materials like polyester and polyurethane. Plus the type of wood used in this section of the remodeled pier. This might help us determine the source of the fire. We should be finished in roughly three hours."

"Contact the front desk when you're done. They'll get hold of me."

The captain went back to his crew.

Gage twisted his shoulders and closed his eyes.

Hiram came over and gave Gage a pat on the back. "Take it easy boss man, they're going to work it all out. Come on, let's make sure all guests are given assurances that we're tackling the problem and the danger is over."

Gage started to speak but his cell phone rang. He looked at the name and number. It was Matt. "Gage, I'm sinking. I just got back and my wife told me that the WSDA called. and said they're sending a team over to check the manure pollution on my farm. They said it seems water running off the manure from my animals, along with bacteria from the animals, might be causing problems with Washington's waters. I have to shut down all operations on the farm till they finish their inspection. This has never happened before. It has to be because of that Dillon character. He wants my farm and he'll bribe any government department to get what he wants. I can't survive. Will you try, really try, and stop this man?" There was a pause on the phone. "My wife's crying. I've got to go and talk to her." Matt hung up.

Gage turned to Hiram. "One mess after another. Obviously your threat didn't do anything. Matt heard today that the WSDA is

31

having him shut down his farm. What's happening in this life?" He shook his hand toward the dining room. "My hotel was starting to crumble. Matt's dream is crumbling. This is a nightmare."

Hiram took Gage over to the wall of windows. "Yes, it's a pisser right now," Hiram said. "But the beauty is, it's only happening RIGHT NOW. You have no idea, no one does, what the future holds. Issues on that timeline are all guess work, planned projections to grasp at security. Instead of dealing with the future, stay in the power of the now without mind-blinders. It doesn't mean we don't fix the damn floor in the banquet room, or find out what caused the eruption in the first place. And it doesn't mean we don't fix Matt's problem. It means, we do it all with a cool teen, high sign."

"A what?"

"We don't attach to any fears and worries, because they're just thoughts. They ain't real. So we let 'em go, with a fuck-you finger, and keep letting them go—till they're out of our minds. Then we deal with what's in front of us, with spunk, spirit, and a gallon of grit."

Gage looked at Hiram as though he had fog in his eyes, and then started to smile.

"Now get on upstairs Gage, and do some Buddha breathing. I'll help with the firefighters, then I'll call Tony D."

Simmons walked into Gage's upper office wearing a polished pencil skirt and ruffled his hair. She sat down next to him and looked out toward the bay. It was spectacular as always. "I just got back from Bellingham and thought I might take a chance and see if you were here, instead of driving straight to the house. Front desk was pretty active, but they did say you were here. What's going on with all the commotion?"

"There was a fire in the banquet room floors. It was just about dinner time, and the guests jumped into panic mode. The Fire Department came and put out the fire. Now they're searching for the cause. The guests are still confused, but Hiram is calming it all down. I was going over the top, so he sent me up here to meditate." Gage held her hand. "And to make it all worse, Matt called and he's pretty fearful. The WSDA is going to shut down his farm due to some stupid thing about manure pollution. It's never happened before in all the years he or his father has had the land. It looks as though that corporate farmer is somehow bribing the WSDA to get Matt to throw in the sponge and hand over his farm. Simmons, I've got to stop Matt from being hurt. His heart is gold, his farm is genuine, and his goals are realistic, filled with a foundation for the family."

She hugged him tenderly.

"The thing is, Hiram and Anna went over to this Dillon Russell and tried to persuade him to stop going after Matt, and to find out who Russell is bribing in our state government. Hiram even gave a pretty sharp threat. But Dillon apparently disregarded the whole talk. I need to find out who he's bribing and use it against him, so he'll leave Matt alone. But time is getting tight, and I'm feeling pretty edgy."

Simmons kept holding his hand.

Hiram walked in. "Howdy Simmons, they told me you were here. It's great to see you. Gage, the guests are all settled down. We're opening the small lunch room and getting the kitchen geared up for tomorrow. The fire guys are rubbing hard to get some clues as to what triggered the damn flames."

Hiram sat down next to Gage with his head held high. "Tony D got back to me. And yes, this Dillon guy has weaknesses like we all do. He didn't know how much he needed his wife until she started having an affair. Her cheating lasted a couple months. Finally she told Dillon she was leaving him. He wouldn't hear of it. He begged her not to leave, to drop the affair, and come back to their marriage. She wouldn't do it. Two days later Dillon had her boyfriend smashed close to death. His wife was shattered. She went into a coma for almost a week, but slowly responded and realized the god-awful truth: her affair was only a temporary thing. Her boyfriend was just a way to get a break from Dillon's temper. And even though Dillon's temper vacillated, he had bright qualities she enjoyed. Dillon loved to be next to her, and every night he touched her arms and legs softly as they made dinners together. He also worshiped the sun and sea as much as she did. Then the hopscotch of life blasted things apart: she was killed in a car accident. He loved his wife beyond measure. And, believe it or not, Simmons, not Anna, looks somewhat similar to his wife."

Gage squinted both eyes.

Simmons also looked surprised.

"Last point: Tony unraveled that Dillon is addicted to gambling and jazz. He goes to the Northern Quest Casino every Saturday night—stays till closing."

Simmons jumped from her chair. "It takes no club brain to get what you're going to say

Hiram." She turned to Gage. "And, I can do this Gage. Anna's not the only one who attracts men. I can blind this Dillon's eye with passion, and gain the information you need from him."

"Simmons, sit down. Don't even look down that road. The man lives way over in

Spokane. You can't go over to Spokane, walk into a nightclub, and strut your sex. They'll—"

"Damn right I can! You want that information. I can be seductive and have him tell me who he's bribing, or I'll find the information in another way. Somehow, someway, I'll get the facts."

"That's crazy! If you'd stop for a few seconds, you'd realize—"

"You need the name to help Matt out of death's door. If he doesn't get to keep the farm, his whole life will be shattered."

"Yes, but I can't have you get hurt for helping me. Period! This Dillon character is known for being a brute, and he could harm you if you make one mistake. Got it?"

Simmons walked over to Gage. "Dear, I know this is tense for all of us. But your Matt is stuck in quicksand and sinking fast. You've helped me, you've helped Anna and Hiram, and more than half the staff at The Inn. Now it's my turn, and Hiram's and Anna's, to help you with this family farmer, and do it quickly."

"Simmons! I'm not going to have you stuck in a doorway of difficulty. We'll think of another way to—"

"Gage," Hiram crushed his cigarette on the desk, "stay loose, stay awake. What's that quote you have on your office wall? 'I'm too positive to be doubtful, too optimistic to be fearful, and too determined to be defeated.' Let Simmons do it."

"You egg-head! That's about perseverance; that's not about love. Simmons cannot be asked to enter into such a risky situation."

"Sweetheart," Simmons said, "life always involves risks and uncertainties. Isn't that what your Buddha boy keeps saying? It's not about having things predicable and buttoned down tight. Even ordinary sex can be risky, if you found out later that the person you were in bed with had hepatitis. Gage, I'm willing to take this shot in the dark for you, and for a man that has helped both of us. Please let me in on this adventure. I can do this!"

How could he even consider this? Both Simmons and The Inn were his soul mates. They gave him courage. They gave him the passion to pursue past his uncertainties. They helped him dream the impossible. He couldn't let either one be subject to harm.

Good thoughts Gage, the deeper part of his brain said, but you're forgetting one thing: Simmons wants to grow, and gain courage like you. And how do you help her do that? By letting her take risks. That's the way all heroines and heroes develop, and get to walk with wonder through this tunnel called life. Give her this opportunity.

Quickly some eerie images from the past started appearing within him. Gage began to remember something that happened one snowy night at a tall wall as he was running away from his private school. He'd been ridiculed and laughed at for his ASD in the school long enough. He couldn't—he wouldn't—take it anymore. He had started climbing up and over the giant wall surrounding the school when a hand had grabbed his collar and brought him down from the long-limbered wall. The tall teacher took his hand off of Gage and said, 'Never. Never run from fear little guy. Face your fears and get to know your true self. Then see what happens. Come on back to school with me Gage, and learn to approach the kids that pick on you for stuttering. I'll help you. I'm the coach of lacrosse. Join my team tomorrow, and I'll start showing you how to change your life—and become one hell of a top dog, that never quits.'

Gage's eyes became wet and wondrous. He looked at Hiram, then at Simmons. "Actually Simmons, you'll be perfect for this wild show of getting Dillon to spill the beans. Hiram, will you give her some facts on Dillon, and what he looks like, and some backup lessons on deceit and deception that can be used on Dillon."

"One more piece of info," Hiram said. "Tony says that his wife always wore a small glass ring with blue-green alga embedded into it. Definitely unique. As Tony's contact said, 'It had a subtle emanation of joy flowing through it.' I think Simmons would look sharp wearing a rock block like that."

CHAPTER 7

Cindy was holding their baby as she and Matt were outside on the porch. It was a beautiful day, and the farmland and mountains were outstanding. "Matt, what are we going to do if the WSDA shuts down the farm completely? I'm worried about money. We're barely existing and Jenny—she held the baby tightly—is going to need more exams, and our sons are growing up quickly. They need new clothes. Besides bikes and books. We're draining most of our savings. What are we going to do?"

"We'll get through this. This Gage McClure is working like a wild dog to stop Dillon's action and the WSDA threats. I'll start working as a part-time carpenter to keep the farm above water. As for the farm money, I've found that apples, tomatoes, and grapes, sundried and in portable form, are selling pretty well. And, people pay more for items like goat milk when it comes concentrated into a soap. It'll take some good work, but I'm sure we'll start to see some good profit as I push into these projects. We just have to weather this 'shut down' storm." Matt held her hand and smoothly rubbed their little child.

"Matt, you have creativity, but our situation is horrible. I'm really starting to think we should get out of farming. We're barely making a living and we've got three children. The whole economy has shifted since your father had the farm, and there are many giant farms taking over this part of the economy. Please, let us move. We can go to my sisters in New Jersey and find work there."

"Cindy, what are you talking about? Leave this land? Leave the horses, the cattle, the crops, and this view?" He waved his hand across the horizon. "There is no way we'll do that. Our sons are going to inherit this beauty. More and more family farmers are being displaced and replaced by chemicals and machines, and political power. We won't cave into those pressures. Small is beautiful! We'll persevere with hard work and heart. We'll keep our courage and live life. This earth, right here, is our Eden. We will not lose it!"

"Matt, your passion is intense, that's noble, that's the reason I'm so attracted to you—but now we have children. We have a responsibility. We can't dream away our obligation and duty. We don't need to become rich; we simply need to keep our promise: we will protect our children. We are not stupid parents. We need to sell this place and get real jobs."

Matt closed his eyes for a moment. "Cindy, this isn't about making sense. It's about honor. Sure, if we stay on the farm and work like hell, we may fail, maybe for months! But failure is more beneficial than most people think. It's one of the biggest ways to learn and grow as we move to our goal of familyhood, farming, and fun. What about that weird man, years ago, Thomas Edison. His teachers called him "stupid," and he was fired multiple times before inventing the light bulb. We can reach our dream to farm and to protect our children. Cindy, we can do this as a team." He got up, walked over, and kissed her softly and delicately.

She hugged him back. "Matt, I love you so much. And, yes, this farm is beautiful."

"Mommy, daddy," little Tommy yelled from the door. "The water! It's all gone. There is none."

"What do you mean, Tommy?"

"I wanted to get a glass of water so I turned on the kitchen faucet. Nothing came out. I tried in the bathroom, nothing."

Matt got up and went to the kitchen. He tampered with the faucets. No water. He ran outside to the deep well in back of the barn. As he ran, gun shots came from inside the barn, and out walked four men in tailored suites.

Tommy and Billy ran to mommy. Cindy quickly held them. Her eyes were wide open, and her eyebrows were raised high.

"Mr. Hastings," the lead man said as he walked toward Matt. "Your water is gone. Your well is dry. That's bad news. You might say, that's why Mr. Russell is creating a massive irrigation system for the Cle Elum area. He needs your land for such a system to be developed, and make sure all his properties will be protected." The man reached inside his coat. "It's a check for double the value of your property. Take it, and we'll be out of your way. Don't take it and you're going to face severe trouble." The man handed Matt the envelope.

Matt refused the envelope. "Why don't you leave? Russell and I have had similar talks. As always I've said, no. This is a family farm. It will go to my sons. Now get out of here, or I'm calling the cops. Or, you can shoot me." Matt turned and walked back to the house. Hell, wonder if they'd shoot him? Would his family survive? Was he simply being defiant that he had to be right and they had to be wrong? Turn around! Take the check. You'll be able to buy a house in Spokane and you can be a carpenter full time. The family will be safe.

"Stop your demented demeanor, turn around Mr. Hastings."

No, he wouldn't turn around. He wouldn't take any money from these idiots. He needed passion to persevere and save the farm; he'd generate it, and he would find ways to win out. He got to the porch. Cindy looked even more frightened than before, and his sons had their eyes closed. They held her dress tightly. As he started to walk up the steps, he heard the car engine, and then he saw the car drive past the barn and out the gate.

CHAPTER 8

It was a sultry Saturday night in downtown Spokane, and Simmons was walking into The Northern Quest Casino. Hiram had given her a picture of Dillon Russell before she left Seattle. The casino was filled with soft lights, guests, and gamblers. Constant conversations, along with a steady rhythm of laughter, filled the room. And the small stage had a chorus line of talented ladies waving their dresses while dancing to lively saxophone music.

As she sauntered through the room several men gazed at her. She knew it wasn't simply her laced-up dress; it was the way the dress accented her best features. Hmm, maybe she should go into the business Anna had to exit: high-end prostitution? Simmons giggled for a second.

She came to one of the blackjack tables where Dillon Russell appeared to be enjoying the thrill of the game. There was a large crowd around the table as all the players were competing with the dealer. Stacks of chips were in front of many of the players, but Dillon had the biggest pile. Simmons watched for over ten minutes. Dillon definitely seemed to have an instinct for firm betting and card counting. And he used it all wisely. As Tony told Hiram, Dillon would not change his bets too often, but now and then he would make a stupid play to make sure the pit boss didn't get suspicious of his card counting.

For another half an hour Dillon kept up the competition, then nodded to the dealer and the four other players as he got up. Simmons had already placed herself in his way as he turned to leave for the table. Bang. Oops! He bumped right into the top part of her laced-up dress. She jumped to purposely have his shoulder tear the lace lining and reveal her left breast. Quickly she covered her breast with her right hand and inhaled. Dillon immediately took off his suit coat and wrapped it around her. "Ma'am, I'm terribly sorry. I didn't see you. I've—"

"Look what you've done."

Many people turned around and gazed at Simmons.

"I really am sorry."

"Sorry! You're a rude man. And stop looking at my bosom!" Simmons started to leave.

Dillon gently held her arm. "Ma'am, I've spent so much time at the game table I must of become blurry-eyed. Please let me—" Dillon looked down at Simmons' ring and stared for a moment.

"What? Why are you looking at my hand?" Simmons stomped on the floor and started to walk away.

Dillon was a little red in the face, but immediately composed himself. He held Simmons once more, turned, and waved for a waitress. The girl rushed over to them. "Please take this lady to Miss Jennings, and have her sew up the torn part of her dress. Then have Miss Jennings escort her to the upper landing. I'll be at the corner table."

The waitress escorted Simmons to the service manager's office. Later she was escorted back to Dillon Russell. As she sat down, Dillon handed her a glass of Dom Pérignon. "Well, this has certainly been a whirlwind Miss—excuse me, what is your name?"

"Emelda Reynolds," Simmons said.

"Emelda, this has all been my fault. My actions made you embarrassed and mad." He clicked their glasses. "Never, will I do this again to any lady."

"Never, say never Mr.—and what is your name?"

"Dillon Russell." He sipped more champagne. "I come here often to settle down from the week's work."

"And what work do you do?"

He half smiled. "I work in land investments."

"What kind?"

"Your normal run of the mill. I come to the casino to—"

"You can't give me a straight answer?" Simmons got up from her chair and started to leave.

Dillon quickly responded and dashed around the table. He held Simmons' shoulder. "Miss Reynolds, please don't leave just yet. I'd like us both to calm down."

"Normal run of the mill? That means nothing. You've either had too much to drink, or you waste your time being trite. I need to leave."

"Land investments, Miss Reynolds. I buy selective farming properties to try and create farming on a better scale. I farm to avoid agricultural waste and create a better quality in production. Unfortunately, many people are against large farm owners. But I'm not blinded by those opinions. I love farming; I love the land and the security it provides."

Simmons pretended to be patient. Hiram was right. Dillon was a smooth-talking con man. He wants me, or anyone, to not believe the only reason he's doing all this is for one reason: quarterly profits. He doesn't mention that he creates environmental disaster through excessive pesticides and soil erosion, and that he's eliminating the livelihoods of small farmers and producers by using government subsidies. He's destroying the fabric of rural America. And he's destroying Matt Hastings.

"I've never stepped onto a farm," Simmons said, "but I've seen pictures in Time and Newsweek. Yes, farmlands do look gorgeous. Seems you've chosen the right work, Mr. Russell."

Dillon half-smiled, but suddenly looked puzzled, again. "Emelda, may I ask, where did you get the ring you're wearing? I haven't seen that kind of a ring on anyone, except my wife who . . . who passed away last year."

"I was hiking along Clear Lake one day. While I stopped for a while I noticed an outrageous mixture of blue and green algae along the shoreline. I couldn't believe their soft charm. I was stunned by the glamour and grace of nature, so I went into the lake and carefully took a handful and put them in a glass bottle I used for drinking water. When I got back home I asked a girlfriend, who worked in ceramics, if she could make some kind of transparent ring with a daring replica of the algae I collected, and then place the thin replica into the ring. It took her almost half a year, given her other priorities, but she finally did it." Simmons held her hand in the air. "Its beauty helps me get through the tough times."

"Emelda, you do amaze me. The ring my wife wore actually did the same thing for her, and at times, for me also." Dillon looked down at the table for a moment. "I certainly don't say this to most women, but, somehow, you're irregular and mystifying; you're a different kind of lady." He drank some champagne. "My wife's death was a disaster for me. She was the dearest person in my life. Yes, we had disagreements at times, but we always patched things up. After the last argument, Kathren and I slammed doors and yelled. But we made up and got back on the good road. Then all hell broke loose: she was killed in a car accident." He mumbled a little. "I still haven't recovered from the loss or the loneliness."

"A friend of mine," Simmons said," a guy who's more real than most of us, says that we usually regard loss and loneliness as an enemy. Heartache is not something we choose to invite in. It's fluid with all kinds of butterflies, and hot with the desire to escape and find something or someone to keep us company again. But my friend says, why not try a different approach? Why not just sit with the feelings of loss for a good ten minutes? Sit with them, but don't attach to them. He says if we have the courage to do this, the feelings lessen, and just go away. You're no longer trying to drive forward while keepin' your car in reverse."

Dillon looked baffled and starry-eyed, all at the same time. "Emelda, are you some kind of a shrink?"

"No, I go to meditation classes a little, and I listen to that ace buddy of mine when he tries to help."

Dillon almost laughed. "Fascinating. I mean it."

He glanced down at his watch. "It's getting late. I want to get back to my house and relax in the sauna. Miss Reynolds, would you be my guest for the night? My house has several bathrooms with saunas; I'd love to share one with you. But if you need to be alone, I'll appreciate that. We can get a good night's sleep, and my cook will make a scrumptious breakfast we can eat out on the deck." Dillon leaned over and gave Simmons an inviting kiss on the cheek. "Come on, let's go."

This was the part she was skittish about. Sure, she was good at attracting his interests; hell, she had the looks of Anna. But how was she going to get the names of the people in the WSDA? How was she going to have him open up without having to undress in front of him? She wouldn't have sex. This is the nightmare that made her cringe. Oh God, she would not have this man pinch her bra or squeeze her—No!

She tugged at her dress. What is it that Gage keeps repeating? 'I'm too determined to be defeated. I won't quit.' He even breaks down in tears sometimes when he says this. But he's built the greatest hotel on Seattle's waterfront through his strength and stick-to-itiveness. Blast the damn ducks, she'd find a way through this fire and she'd get the information. "Mr. Russell, you're a bit presumptuous, but amusing. Yes, let's go."

Behind Dillon's private gates a wonderland appeared. Two big boulder-style waterfalls, with bubbling blue waters, guided their way through the estate, which was surrounded by rich gardens and delicately groomed hedges. Heaters lined the walkways running in front of the waterfalls and all the way up to the main door. Inside, the foyer set the tone for this magnificent mansion. It was thick with polished travertine floors, master crafted with natural stone, and lit with crystals. Nothing was overlooked, nothing was an after-thought. The paintings on the wall quickly collared Simmons' attention. It was a light show filled with rapturous reds, brilliant yellows, many shades of greens, and bursts of blues. This place was inviting, expansive, and warm. And, for God's sake, there was even a fish tank in the main room with colorful fish swimming everywhere along the whole length of the wall.

"Do you care for a drink?" Dillon asked.

"No, but I would like to take a hot bath, and then meet you by the fireplace in your living room." Simmons pointed to the far room.

"Of course." Dillon went over to mahogany desk and pressed a button. Moments later a servant appeared and escorted Simmons to a bedroom.

After the bath, she dried off and flopped onto the bed. She was refreshed and rejuvenated. Now, how to get the names? He wouldn't just tell her the names. She had to—wait! He must have an office in this massive palace. Of course he had his downtown office, but wouldn't he also have an additional one in this palace? Couldn't she find out where it was? She got up, tied a thick robe around her, put on her glass ring, and walked down to the living room. The fish were floating and gliding along the wall, and the fireplace was beaming brightly.

Dillon got up from the sofa and welcomed her in. "You do look uplifting, Emelda."

She sat down next to him. Her robe lifted way past her thighs. She needed to arouse him just a little. She couldn't go too far. Thank god there were other people in the house. The servant told her there were five other attendants living in the house. "Dillon, I think it's my turn to be amazed by you. This … this chateau of yours is out of a movie. How many bedrooms are there?"

"Six bedrooms, eight baths."

"What about the other rooms here?"

"Emelda, a mansion is not so much defined by how many rooms it has but more by the fact that rooms are created and designed for specific purpose. Here I have a home theater room, a billiard room, an infinity pool, and a library. Of course, there's the formal dining room, the formal living room we're in, a sitting room, the foyer with the art work, as well as my grand master suite, and the bedrooms and bathrooms we've already mentioned."

"Why would you ever want to leave this beautiful place and go to work or meetings at your downtown company? Can't you work right here?"

"Actually, I do split my time between the Financial Center and home. I've got an office down here, and up in the east wing."

All right! She was getting close to the gate! "Dillon, you're living in paradise. OK, I'm dead tired. I'm calling it quits and will join you for a delicious breakfast. Afterwards, can we walk around the grounds and go down by the river?" She kept rubbing the glass ring.

"Emelda," Dillon moved closer. "I've got to tell you something." He rubbed her thigh. Simmons felt as nervous as a new witch on a broom. She was not going to open up her robe. "I'd love to go to bed with you; I'd like to hug you all night, but I can see you're tired."

Simmons forced a cute smile. "Let's put it on the calendar for tomorrow night, OK?

He smiled back. "Let me walk you up to your room, then meet you for breakfast, and tomorrow I will show all around the estate."

Late into the night, Simmons quietly opened her bedroom door, tiptoed down the hallway and proceeded over to the east wing. She started to open the door to the first room when a servant started to turn into the hallway. She immediately looked for a place to hide—there! There was a small nook on the other side of the hallway. She tucked herself into the opening, hoping like a horny-ass pig the servant would go down the stairway instead of walking straight ahead. Yes! He was going down the stairs.

Simmons carefully opened the door to the first room and flicked on her small flashlight. No, this was no office. It was more like a music room with a baby grand piano. She slowly shut the door and softly moved down the hallway, always looking for any more servants or security. She opened a second door. It was a study room with wooden paneled walls, book shelves from floor to ceiling, and several red leather chairs on wheels. She walked in and looked around. No, this couldn't be an office. There was only one desk with no drawers and just a thin notebook lying on top. She opened the notebook. Written into it were quotes from different authors, several esoteric phrases, and some philosophical question without answers; but no people's name, no WSDA references. She closed the notebook and—rats! Someone was coming down the hallway. She turned off the flashlight, closed the door, jetted under the desk, and listened like a vulture. A door across the study room opened and closed, then opened again. The person continued down the hallway. She waited a full five minutes before she left the study room, then she went down the hallway to the next door; slowly opened it, and turned on the flashlight. All right! This was an office.

Simmons shut the door.

The room, like the study room, had wooden paneled walls, but was much more rich looking with its mahogany wood. There were bookshelves on all the walls and a tall window overlooking a beautiful backyard garden. It was a small room but packed to the hilt. The tall desk took up a great deal of room space, along with the carved mahogany file cabinets. There was a computer on the desk, along with different folders, and some high-tech gadgets that had no meaning to her. The huge Kashmir carpet was ravishing and the chandelier was almost ethereal.

Let's see, if she had placed the names somewhere, where would she have put them? Not on top of the desk, and not in the computer—no matter how perfect the laptop was, hackers could always find a way into a computer. No, they'd be beneath or below the desktop, sort of like a hyporheic zone of a river. She laughed at herself. Gage always used that phrase as a metaphor for things that couldn't be seen. She opened several drawers. Nothing. Out of frustration she clumsily slid a notebook in the main drawer to the side. She was sick and tired of—what? On the left side of the drawer the wood tilted and she saw several note cards. She pulled them out. She turned the flashlight onto the cards. They had hand written names of products, companies, and—mother fucker! One of the cards had WSDA written on the top. In the middle of the card was a name with different money amounts next to it, and different descriptions.

All of a sudden the lights came on.

"Stay still, don't even move." The security guard had a gun pointing at her as he walked over and grabbed the cards from her. Then he slapped her face and pushed her onto the chair. He opened his portable, waited for almost a minute, and spoke: "Mr. Russell, a little surprise for you. Your guest broke into your office and has pulled out ID cards relating to the WSDA." He stopped talking; obviously Dillon was giving out orders.

He hung up and turned toward Simmons. "We'll wait."

Dillon pushed the door open, looked around, then walked over to the guard. "Where are the cards?"

The guard handed them to Dillon. "Well, Emelda—if that is your name—you seem to be skilled in deception and sex appeal. What are you? A slut who favors large sums of money for her pussy and perfidy?"

Now what could she do? How was she going to escape this? Would she, could she, escape this? She couldn't be tied up, and fucked, and threatened.

"You want to tell me why you took these cards? Who the hell were you going to give them to?" Dillon slapped her hard.

He turned toward the guard. "Cuff the bitch and bring her with us."

They all walked up to one of the master bedrooms Simmons had been given. The guard pushed Simmons onto the bed as Dillon rifled through her clothes looking for her mobile phone. He found it, and turned it on. Then he hit 'Recent' and looked at the last call she made. There was a name above the number. A name Dillon definitely remembered when a Hiram Smith came to his office to try and persuade him to back off on the Matt Hastings takeover. This Hiram also shot two of his guards.

Dillon tapped the number on the mobile phone. After three rings, a man answered, "Simmons?"

"No, this ain't Simmons. Is this Hiram?"

"Yes. Where's Simmons?"

"She asked me to call you. She's in a little trouble and said the only way out was for you to—"

"HIRAM," Simmons yelled. The guard turned and smashed Simmons in the side of her head.

"What's going on?" Hiram hollered.

"Good question, Hiram. I ask the same thing. Why did your Simmons come over here?"

"What! Who are—"

"Shut the fuck up Hiram. I'm Dillon Russell. But you probably know that. Get smart, and tell me the answer: Why did she come over here?"

"She did it for the same reason Matt Hastings is trying to get out of trouble. You're doing harm to good people and you've got to stop it. You don't, and I'll find ways to burn you in hot water.

"You try anything like that—anything—and your sweet Simmons is going to be harmed. I'll release her as soon as Matt antes up and

49

hands over the farm. Do I make myself clear?" Dillon pushed the off button.

CHAPTER 9

Several guests at the hotel were enjoying themselves in the sauna room when that section of the hotel began to shake like a railroad train on rusty tracks. The guests looked at each other with wide eyes and broken smiles. All of a sudden some of the benches in the sauna room collapsed and crashed to the floor. Two of the guests were trying to hang onto the wall to save themselves, while many others were sprawled over the wooden floor.

The front desk called Hiram. None of the guests were hurt but they were nervous as hell, and he should get down to the sauna room fast.

Hiram was coming out of the main hallway door as Gage was coming down the hall. They both jetted to the sauna where staff members from Guest Service were helping everyone relax, making double sure they were not hurt, and taking them to their rooms. Some of the ceiling lights had split apart, and in the middle of the room, the sauna pools were all cracked.

Cold sweat ran down Gage's face. The hotel was his love; it was his life. He needed The Inn to be double safe and secure. Damn it, his guests were his family. He created the hotel's environment to form a sense of peace and joy for his guests, no matter if they were business execs or simple tourists wanting a break from the normal hustle and bustle of life. The Inn had passion. It gave him freedom from a world masked with pretenses and prejudices that judged and defined everything and everyone. "Hiram, what the hell is going on? Just days ago there was a floor fire in the dining room. We still don't know how it started. That's never happened here! And now the sauna collapses!"

"Have no idea what's going on Gage, but at least there's no fire this goddamn time." Hiram brought Gage closer to the wall. "The head Fire Guy had just gotten back to me from last week's disaster and said many docks and pier fires are caused when the aluminum foil of the building material becomes energized by electricity. He said it was probably some kind of innovative coil gun, powered by electricity that caused our fire. He suggested that someone might have been tampering with the pier. And now, looks like someone's messing with our pier, again."

Gage froze. He hated parts of his life. If he was concentrating on goodwill–why was life throwing crowbars into his warmth and will?

"And to make matters even worse," Hiram said, "I was just about to burst into your office. Simmons has been caught by Dillon. He found out about her disguise and what the hell she was up to. He called me, demanded that Matt antes up, and we leave everything alone, or Simmons will be abused. We definitely need Simmons. So I'm going to call Tony D, find out some strategies, and then go over and have a talk with Dillon. "

"Simmons! She can't get hurt. Hiram, I need her!"

"We'll handle it all Gage. We always have; we always will. Right now, let's see what needs to be put under control in the hotel. Then I'll call Tony."

After they rearranged the sauna for the maintenance crew, Hiram went up to his suite, jerked open the fridge and took out a cold beer. Then he called Tony D. When the man answered Hiram said: "Well, Simmons almost got the info on Dillon Russell's contact with the WSDA, but damn it, she got caught." Hiram went on and told him the whole ball of wax.

Tony spit out some mucus. "Hiram, ya gotta start squeezing things around Dillon's great empire. I found out some private ventures he keeps quiet. Besides his corporate farming endeavor, he's got a maze of car washes and parking lots he uses for a subtle form of money laundering and bribery. He deposits the loose money from these cash cows into the Island Northwest Bank. Because of the Bank Security Act, he can deposit under ten thousand dollars in pure cash without it ever being reported or questioned. And then he draws the cash out, in limited quantities, and puts it into a trust fund he has in the Cook Islands—where it'll never be registered."

Hiram felt like he was entering a casino, with heavy betting, as Tony kept talking.

"So wonder," Tony said, "if you make it known to dear Dillon that you've got clues to all this. And that you'll make a cash deposit of more than ten thousand dollars into his Island Northwest account, if he doesn't listen up. Hiram, if you do it twice, the bank and the Federal Government will send out warrants and warriors to investigate the owner of the account. There goes his resource to bribe people and open up confidential doors. Even if Dillon changes banks after he hears this, I can locate the new bank just like I found this one."

Tony spit out some more mucus. "I'll also try and find out who Dillon is paying off at the WSDA to help him take over small farms. What you want to do is get ready to present all this to Dillon as a swap for Simmons. This info should take enough oxygen out of his bag of bones so he'll easily trade Simmons for a hushed mouth, and stop him from taking over Matt's land. I think you should bring Anna along with you when you visit Dillon. She has some of the same sexual looks as Simmons does. Dillon is a fan for those looks. OK, gotta go." Tony hung up.

Hiram looked out across the waters of Elliott Bay. Its wide open beauty and spectacular view of Mount Rainier were like angels to this blue sky bay.

CHAPTER 10

Vivian came on the intercom. "Gage, a Brice Hafer is on the phone. Something to do with the construction of our pier. He asked for you. Shall I pass him through?"

"All right."

The call rang on his second phone. "Hello, Gage McClure here."

"Mr. McClure, thank you for taking my call. First, I need to tell you, you've got a sharp hotel. I am marveled by the fact that it's the only hotel in Seattle built over the water. I'm amazed that you formed it all with your own creativity. It's got to be worth millions. The only problem is, recently you've been written up in the Seattle Times and the PI that guests are starting to check out of your hotel. It seems your precious Inn isn't too safe. There have been floor fires, and just today your sauna room scared the hell out of your guests as it crumbled and cracked. I'm calling to make a point: I'm the one who's caused all this to happen."

"What!"

"Mr. McClure, cancelations on future reservations will start to appear. You're beginning to get a rather disagreeable reputation. I think it's wise to take some corrective action."

Jesus Christ, what was this guy saying? Yes, there were cancelations, enough to cough up blood. Was Gage so tense that any cutthroat capitalist could sense his hidden hang-ups and find ways to take advantage of them? "Mr. Hafer, do you have any idea how close you are to subpoenas and penalties? All calls on this line are taped and —"

"McClure! If you insist on acting like a blockhead, I'll create more explosions on your famous pier. And more guests will check out. You're in a bind. The only way out is to listen to me and the offer I'm going to give you. Are we clear on this?"

Slow down, Gage's voice yelled. You'll tackle this, just as you tackled that stupid Baxter Group last year. "What exactly is your offer?"

"That you wise up and give me The Inn."

"Get off the phone."

"Plus McClure, I'll give you a total of forty percent of the gross, and another thirty-three percent every year for five years. You'll be set for life. But if you don't accept my office, you'll be ruined for life. And as I said, I'm ready to instigate more damage without you ever knowing where or what. Now before you throw back the insults, think about all this. I'll call you tomorrow at 10 in the morning."

Hafer hung up.

Gage sat back in the chair and remembered another of Hiram's saying: 'Karma, Gage. Cause and effect. What you send out into the world, comes back to ya. Act, yes, but don't overreact.' Hafer wasn't going to ignite another part of The Inn. Gage looked out the window and out toward the bay. What he had to do was assemble some detection cameras throughout the pier, and have his maintenance staff attach the cameras to a private circuit board on a twenty-four seven schedule. Then if Hafer, or one of his men, clandestinely came to the pier, they'd be caught, and maybe even killed. Gage would never let go of The Inn.

After talking to Gage, Brice Hafer made another call to a colleague, Mark Schmit. "Is the damn thing packed up?"

"It's set and ready to go Brice. I understand your intention and will give it my best shot."

"Mark, I got hold of you because you're the king for this kind of caper. I don't want your best shot, I want your total commitment. It's gotta happen, and happen with chaos. Get it nailed down tight, goddamn it."

"For me to screw up the whole waterfront hotel from just one guest room is a high roll. And, it doesn't matter if the five-star is in Seattle, San Diego, or Da Nang I can't guarantee I won't be caught packin' the bomb in place. But I'm going for it."

Brice knew this was a high stake game, but he had no other option. He had to ruin this hotel and two other waterfront properties to get his goal, and achieve the honor his heritage deserved. "Go for it, good guy."

Around midnight, a young married couple checked into The Inn. They were laughing with the desk clerk and excited to go to their water view suite for happiness and pleasure.

"You have an open ticket, how long will your stay be?" asked the clerk as he looked at the reservation.

"We're here on our anniversary. I would think at least five days," the husband said. "Tomorrow when we come down for breakfast will there be someone that could map out the fun stops in Seattle?"

"Absolutely. The morning desk clerk will get you in touch with the concierge. She'll give you maps and insights to the city."

They both smiled like a pair of first graders.

"Here's your key. Take the elevator up to the third floor and keep walking toward your left. Room 307. Have a great night, both of you."

After they went into the room and turned some of the lights on, they walked to a wall of windows. The hotel was warmly embraced by Elliott Bay, and lights reflecting from West Seattle were dancing on the water. Mark turned to Judy. "To bad we have to ruin this night for so many people. This is one remarkable hotel." For a moment, he kept looking out the window. "OK, enough of my irons in the fire, let's get to work."

Judy opened up one of the large suitcases and took out a giant boombox from the luggage. She set the bass and treble controls to the highest level, and set the gain control of the graphic equalizer— the one Mark designed for this project—to its highest level. She then opened another suitcase and took out some speakers. Mark connected the seven creative decibel speakers to the boombox and set the LED sound level to maximum. Meanwhile Judy moved some of the corner tables in the suite and put them in the center of the room.

When everything was finished, they brought three speakers next to an open window and put the other four speakers onto the tables. Then they packed their suitcases, opened the door, and went down the backstairs to their car. After they drove across Alaskan Way they parked under the viaduct, and turned on the boombox by remote. Even though they were way away from the hotel, they could hear the thundering, ear-piercing sound of violent rap music. Judy held Mark's hand tightly as lights went on all over the hotel.

The phones at the front desk started ringing like wild neurons in a glass brain. The night manager quickly called Gage. Gage called security. They had no answer as to where the sounds were coming from but they'd find the source within minutes. "What floor is your team on?" Gage yelled.

"They're on the fifth."

Gage called Hiram and had him meet him at the elevator.

As they got off at the fifth. The noise was deafening. Guests were sticking their necks out of the doorways. Nightgowns and bath-robes clustered the hallway. A security guard was about to get off the elevator, but stopped as he listened to his phone. "It's all coming from the third floor, Gage."

They went down to the third. Two security guards were in front of suite 307. "Why are you guys just standing there? Get the hell in there," Hiram said.

"We've knocked, we can't—"

Hiram pulled out his security key and opened the door. The howling sound was explosive. He ran toward the boombox, smashed it on the floor—and then stomped on it. Suddenly, silence saturated the whole room and hovered along the hallway.

Gage pulled out his cell phone. "Terry, who's registered in 307?" He waited a moment. "Got it. Have they checked out?" Another second passed. "Damn it!" He stuffed the phone back in his pocket.

"What do you want us to do, Hiram?" one of the guards asked.

"Calm everyone down in the hallway. Tell them we're quickly looking into what all this was about. I'll have more men do the same on all floors." Hiram turned toward Gage. "What's the info on this room?"

"Occupied by a married couple. They haven't check out."

Hiram walked back to the boombox and speakers. He picked up the boombox and slowly looked at the controls on the back. All were set to maximum. He also noticed an equalizer. "Gage this rig was hard-wired to the max. What the fuck is going on?"

"That's what I want to know. This is beastly! The guests have to be in an outrage. Come on let's get down to the front desk."

At the front desk things had calmed down a little. The staff at the desk were still answering calls and quieting down angry, rude people. Hiram went over to talk to two mad men in bathrobes and explained what the noise was, and that it had stopped. As Gage was talking with the assistant night manager, a desk clerk interrupted the conversation." Gage, there's a call for you, do you want to take it? It's a Mr. Hafer."

Gage's face tightened as he shook his head. Gage picked up the phone. "Mr. Hafer, now what are you calling about?"

"Don't act stupid, McClure. You've had another can of worms crash through your cherished castle. Your guests are devastated. What do you think the PI or the Seattle Times will say tomorrow about your hotel? Your reputation is coming apart. And, only I can save your soul right now. You've heard my demand: I don't need your hotel as a hotel. I need your hotel to help promote, to help turn around, a god-awful legal verdict that has been allowed to exist in Washington state for years. Hand over your hotel to me; do it before I demolish the place completely. I'll call you again tomorrow to hear your decision." Brice Hafer hung up.

Gage had to protect her, protect The Inn. She was the energy that created empowering realities for him. He was finally becoming what he wanted to be: a man of resource and resolve. Damn it, he had to stop this Hafer guy from harming The Inn. He couldn't go back to the curled up kid that stayed alone at night in his chair, rolled up in his blanket talking to himself about his fears and failures, about not being good enough, not being smart enough, about his stuttering, and his goddamn servility. He had to find a way out of Brice's pressure. Tears started rolling down his cheek.

Hiram came over and turned Gage around. "What's going on good-buddy?"

Gage wiped his face. "Just got off the phone with Brice Hafer. He's the one that's doing all this: the fire on the banquet floors, the sauna, and the sound that crashed through The Inn right now. Again, he said to hand over The Inn to him. He'll give us some kind of cash return. If I don't follow his demand, he'll ruin our hotel and our reputation. And then we'll—"

"Straighten up! He can't crush this hotel. And we've already talked about putting hidden surveillance cameras on the pier, especially underneath the pier, so let's do it! And, we'll increase surveillance on all floors, especially at night. Christ, one nut bag after another wanting our golden palace. We sure ain't gonna hand it over to this Hafer. But right now, let's take care of the guests, then you jump up to your office and do some Buddha breathing."

Gage nodded.

"And while your belly breathing, I'll give Tony D another call, see if he's found the name of the WSDA agent Dillon's been bribing. Even if he hasn't, I'll fly over to Spokane with the other sensitive info on his money laundering, and have another slash session with Dillon. And I'll bring back Simmons. When I return, then we'll tackle the airhead, this Hafer guy."

CHAPTER 11

Hiram entered the Bank of America Financial Center in downtown Spokane. He went up to the 18th floor and walked into Dillon's office. The receptionist recognized him from the last meeting and quickly called for security. Two guards came into the room.

"This man has caused nothing but trouble for Mr. Russell," the receptionist said. "Escort him out of the office and out of this building."

The guards started to grip his arms.

Hiram calmly reached into his pocket and pulled out a sheet of paper, giving it to the receptionist. "Before I leave, I think you need to give this to your Mr. Russell. This might hurt his whole business empire. It would be best if I wait to see if he wants to see me."

The receptionist cautiously left her desk while the guards held Hiram.

Moments later Hiram was escorted into Dillon's office. The guards were ordered to stand outside his office door.

"Well, Mr. Smith, it's not always a pleasure to see you." Dillon looked at the paper once again. "You're getting rather flashy, opening up the backdoor to my privacy and personal procedures. How did you find out about all this?"

"The 'how' is unimportant. Simply stop your actions. Give us Simmons now!"

"Mr. Smith, not only are you inquisitive, but you seem to be a formidable challenge to my goals. However—" Dillon sat down at his desk and turned on the large flat panel screen. All of a sudden screams came out of the wall speakers. The screen was showing Simmons being sexually abused by two men in less than three minutes.

"However, if you don't want to see Simmons groped and molested any further, I doubt you'll choose to continue with your plans. Am I right? I suggest you cancel any further inquiry into my finances, and you should excuse yourself now," Dillon said with a half smile.

"Sharp Dillon, except for one thing: to keep doing your stuff, to keep buying private lands with secret leveraging, you need to continue bribing state and county officials. And the only way to do that is to continue taking money from your chain of car washes you have in three states, and keep that loose cash out of sight from the IRS in an offshore trust, which you're already doing. Your offshore trust is nestled in the Cook Islands, just south of the Hawaiian Islands."

Dillon shifted a little in his chair.

"And, as I found out," Hiram said, "that offshore trust, called the Cook Islands Trust, is a corporation with the strongest reputation for confidentiality and protection. They guard client's assets severely. No one has penetrated the protective shield they have for clients... until recently. This year the Cook Islands' government is getting ready to accept OECD demands, for the first time ever. They, and almost every offshore financial center in the world, will give out information on foreigner's accounts when tax evasion and corruption can be proven. The OECD, based in Paris, France, created stinging strategies so offshore countries would comply with this demand. Hardly anyone knows about it yet. But, it's gonna kill you."

Hiram focused on Dillon's eyes. "You getting the point? When corruption can be proven, offshore banks will open any trust account to the OECD. Fines and prison penalties will follow."

Dillon was definitely losing his cool.

Hiram took out another sheet of paper and laid it on the desk. It had Dillon's name and some of Dillon's financial history. "Man called Tony D is accumulating your financial activities from the past: when you did things legal, and when you started to go over the limits—especially not paying taxes. Once all this information is accumulated, he can release it, and the dear Cook Islanders will be forced to comply with the OECD. There goes your money haven, and here comes your jail time. Get it? You give us Simmons right now. And stop trying to take Matt's farm. Do both of these, and Tony D ain't going to give your illegal history away. You'll be free to quickly rearrange your good old days of deceit before any law targets you."

Dillon looked placidly up toward the ceiling, and then closed his eyes. "You're abrasive, Hiram. But damn savvy. OK, your deal's accepted."

Dillon got on the phone. "Have the lady dressed and delivered to my office."

Hiram kept quiet. Dillon worked on his computer.

Soon, a side door opened and two men held Simmons' arms as she walked in. Or tried to walk in. She was moving in awkward steps. Her clothes were torn and stripped; her face was bloodied and bruised. She tried to smile. "Hirvm. I weed you." She shook her head. "I vean . . . I . . . need you." She started to dash toward him, but stumbled, falling straight onto the floor.

Hiram ran to her and held her tightly. "Simmons." He lifted her up and into his arms. Then he turned to Dillon, started to say something, but didn't. He just stared at the bastard with hate and hostility before he walked out the door with Gage's angel.

While Gage was waiting to hear from Hiram on the success or failure with Dillon, Vivian interrupted him as he was trying to concentrate on a hospitality report. "A Brice Hafer is on the phone, do you want to speak to him?"

Not again! "Yes, pass him through."

"Mr. McClure, we need to meet on Pier 52. I'll be there in an hour. Show up or your hotel is gone for good, and I'm not just talking fires or loud sounds as before. We'll talk about a potential disaster that's going to circle your hotel."

They met close to the Seattle Ferry terminal. "Glad you came, Mr. McClure. Let's take a walk to the far post and have a look at the city."

As they walked Gage turned toward the horizon. Was Brice playing high stakes poker, again? Gage slapped his leg. Was Gage cursed to attract corruption into his life? Last year there was the mess with Arturo. This year, Dillon. And now this mad man.

"Mr. McClure, I'm here to help you, or rather, to save your ass. My team is getting ready to blow apart your pier if you don't take my offer. The explosion will last only sixty seconds and will take place underwater."

"What! What the hell did you just say? Brice, we've installed infrared imaging systems all over the place since your last performance. You'll be detected and trapped if you attempt anything like that."

"I said, underwater, McClure. Any surveillance down there is always distorted, since real time monitoring isn't possible. Any recorded data can't be assessed until the instruments are recovered. You'd never have time enough to be warned."

This man was a monster. Gage's whole life was tied to The Inn. And Hiram's life was too, along with Anna. "Why are you even suggesting this? Why do you make these threats?"

"Right now, it's my business to take your hotel. But you keep trying to resisting my request."

"I'm leaving!"

"McClure, did you think you'd ever get written up in the Times as being irresponsible with your Inn for all the damage that has been done? Of course not. I did the damage, and I'm focused on a twenty-four carat goal. I will succeed. Now, my offer: have a written contract made up, saying you're turning your hotel over to me. You don't, and I'll have your pier demolished. Are we clear?"

"Skip the insanity. You're foolish as hell. Why are you even mentioning this?"

"Ever hear of a man called Schweabe?"

"What? Who?"

"You arrogant man. You've got the best setup in Seattle and you don't even know the history of who helped create this area. Schweabe was the father of Sealth, which, of course, is a Suquamish Indian name. Sealth was the chief of the Suquamish and the Duwamish Indians. The white faces long ago called him Seattle—Chief Seattle—because they didn't have the fuckin' patience to learn any Native American language. And they named this city after him. His correct name was Chief Sealth. But look around, this city is called Seattle, not Sealth. And like most white faces, you hide your ignorance."

This was crazy. Gage pushed Brice aside, and started walking toward the street.

Brice grabbed Gage, and pulled him back by his jacket. Gage tripped and fell. "Hostility started to break out," Brice said, "as more and more goddamn settlers came to the Puget Sound region in the mid 1800s. Whenever white men wanted Indian land, the tribes were pushed farther west. If the Indians protested, they were destroyed with force."

Gage wanted to leave. He needed to.

Brice gave Gage a push. "A treaty was signed by Chief Seattle. Sure, the treaty preserved some Indian rights, but it took away farm land, lakes, and Puget Sound land from the Indians. The treaty was abusive. Chief Leschi, chief of the Nisqually Indians, protested the treaty! To add to his outrage, he affirmed that the Europeans had brought more than greed with them, they brought flu, and measles, and other diseases. The sickness was starting to kill seventy, eighty percent of the Native American population.

"In 1855, Leschi traveled to the territorial capital at Olympia to dispute the terms of the treaty. Acting Governor Charles Mason ordered that Leschi and his brother Quiemuth be taken into custody. Leschi escaped and became war chief in command of three hundred men, creating raids against the white population; and thereby initiating the Puget Sound War from 1855 to 1856."

"Why the hell are you telling me all this? I don't need to know it. I sure don't need you. Get out of here. I'm going back to my hotel."

"Your hotel? You're gonna give me your hotel."

"You are completely nuts."

"Shut up you fool, and listen. As I said, Chief Seattle stayed friends with the white settlers and signed the stupid treaty at Mukilteo. Chief Leschi, on the other hand, kept hammering away at the greed of the government and the destruction of his people. He decided to see the governor again. Sure, he'd surrender some his tribe's land and land rights, as long as Washington State would return the favor with much better peace talks. Many thought he was doing and saying the right thing. And, damn it, he was.

"But Governor Mason didn't think so. He wanted Leschi wiped off the map. He was causing too much turmoil, and actually getting people to see the fallacy of the ridiculous treaty. Chief Leschi was caught and hanged in 1858 for a questionable murder during the war."

Brice kicked his foot on the pavement.

"Why am I telling you this? My blood comes from the Nisqually Indians. Chief Seattle, who certainly was not Nisqually, was praised. And still is. Chief Leschi, head of the Nisqually, was brave and fought for freedom, but was not praised by the government. His hanging is still being debated as if it was the right thing to do. That was almost 200 years ago. I'm going to step up to the plate and have the city of Seattle, along with the fuckin' government, pay a steep price for their madness. Besides taking over your hotel and have it honor Chief Leschi in different ways, I'm going to start wrecking the Seattle waterfront as a fucking penalty they need to pay for."

Damn the gods. To hell with Seattle's history from the past. This guy has no concern, no caring for anything that stands in the way of his obsession. Gage kept looking at the smirk on Brice's face. Shit. OK, calm down. You'll get out of this mess. Not sure how, but you will.

"I want a copy of the contract," Brice said, "that states you're handing your hotel over to me so I can do anything I want with it to promote Leschi. If you don't sign it, your pier will be exploded, and your hotel and guests will be dead meat. Legs and lumber will be flying in the air. Tomorrow McClure, at noon. We meet right here." Brice walked away.

Gage slowly looked over to Pier 67. His hotel was bright and golden, but his eyes were wet and swollen.

When he got back to the hotel Anna told him that Hiram was on his way back. They both hurried downstairs. Soon the hotel car drove up to the door with Hiram and Simmons in it. Simmons was wrapped snuggly in a hotel blanket. Gage opened the door and grabbed hold of her.

"Oh my God, Gage, the horror I've been through. They stripped me naked. They had gorilla sex with me, and it was all put on video. Yes, I was in pain. Yes, I felt like an ancient slave girl for some evil king." She hugged him even tighter. "But the worst fear was that I would be distant from you for the rest of my life."

"Simmons, you've got me. We'll never be separated. And this will never happen again. I want—"

Anna came in from the other side of the vehicle. "Simmons!" Anna started crying.

"Don't ever go on a black-novel trip like this one without me. Never!" She kissed Simmons' neck, and grabbed Gage and hugged him hard.

Now Simmons was crying.

Hiram wiped her face and held the three of them with his long arms and thick hands.

They took a quick elevator up to Gage's private suite.

"Safe, at last," Simmons said.

"We'll be by your side forever," Hiram said, as he took her into the bedroom.

Gage kept holding her hand.

Simmons kept holding his hand. She could never go through this horror again. He had tried to convince her that she should not go after Dillon, no matter what Hiram suggested. Instinctively she felt he was right, but she had pushed away that hunch and insisted on doing it. The love for Gage was always a flame of life that moved her. Deep down, she knew she'd survive. Or hoped she would.

Gage gave her a gentle kiss.

Soft and silent, the lights went off as she drifted into sleep.

CHAPTER 12

Dillon Russell flew over to Rarotonga, in the Cook Islands. He had set up an appointment with Jon Ngaire, Managing Director of the Cook Islands Trust. After a few minutes sitting in the waiting room, he was escorted into Mr. Ngaire's office.

"Mr. Russell, it's been quite a while since we've met, always a pleasure to see you."

"I hear the OECD is initiating some kind of a checkup on tax evaders," Dillon said.

"It's a new request demanding investigation, and detention if needed."

"That's the reason I came," Dillon said, "I'm taking my money out from the trust. I also need a complete wipe out of any trace that I have been associated with your trusts and LLCs."

"Mr. Russell, your activity, like any foreign client, is intertwined in paperwork, investments, purchases, and closeouts. We couldn't unravel all your stockpile of exploits and efforts. Nor is it our job. Our job is—"

"Your job is to serve me. The guy that pays you a heavy ticket for your services."

"We do serve you, Mr. Russell, but we don't wrap ourselves up in unnecessary irascibility and confusion. We concentrate on one thing: helping our clients make big money. All over the world we're known for this. "

"Yes, your name and your company's name has always been mentioned among my friends. But now I need extra help. I've been with you for over eight years, paying you a hefty load of commission. I need your men to roll up their sleeves, look at my limited partnerships, my hedge funds, and all my other investments, and clear out the ways I've avoided paying US taxes."

"Mr. Russell, you're a shrewd man. Keep your common sense tight. We stamp our fiduciary promise very hard: we provide the best quality of investment and asset management, compared to any other trust company. However, we're not a high-tech company. We can take away your records, but we can't guarantee that all the fine details can be gotten rid of. You need to take your funds and dispense—"

Dillon opened his vest pocket, took out a certificate, laid it down on the table, and pushed it over to Mr. Ngaire. "It's new, but not on the market yet."

Mr. Ngaire looked at the red letters on the report.

"As you probably know, log files, " Dillon said, "are the most common technique for any system administrator to determine what has taken place in their system. All logins are put into log files. And when you need to select and erase any logins or logouts from past years, you can now do all the fine details with this, and do it effectively." Dillon pointed to the paper Mr. Ngaire was now holding in his hand. "It's new from MicroPilot, and it has a script called Cleantrim to clear out any log file you want. It's uniquely designed to not just take out information, but it creates a corporate history for you through special codes. You can keep those special codes or discard them whenever you want."

Dillon pulled out a Cleantrim disk and slid it over to Mr. Ngaire. "I'm sure this'll be of value to you in the future." Dillon said. "But right now, Mr. Ngaire, why don't you get your staff to start spending several weeks checking and double checking all my financial trans-actions within your system. Then delete each one of them so there's no evidence of any tax evasion. And, don't mention anything about me to any stupid government. Agreed?"

"Interesting." Mr. Ngaire looked at the disk. "Yes, we'll do what you've asked, but of course, if a government official asks about you, I'll have to comply. I won't test their authority. I won't have my cor-poration questioned."

Dillon smiled. "Your cash hound clients, The Keelson Group and the Jarred Company you thrive on, seem to be a little on the edgy side of justice Mr. Ngaire. Yet you have no objections about not tell-ing any complete story about them to anyone, including the British and American governments. And, you seem to appreciate the hefty bonuses they give you."

Mr. Ngaire looked sternly at Dillon for a moment. "It seems you're well informed Mr. Russell. But I don't want to travel that road. I think you should leave now."

"All I'm doing is letting you know I'm aware of some of the con-cealed actions and accounts surrounding your island enterprise. I'm impressed and I want to keep dealing with you; I'd like you to keep dealing with me."

"Mr. Russell, your personality seems to be getting, shall I say: dis-tasteful. If you keep shoving, we'll shove back with our pressure and power." Mr. Ngaire gave an angry look, but suddenly—he smiled a little. "However, I do see how you've become so very wealthy. You analyze and appraise pretty thoroughly. OK, I'll have my staff work the long hours to shred all your information. We will not mention you or your activities to anyone."

Dillon pressed his lips. The asshole hates me, but he'll go for the long haul. The OECD won't find anything, and Hiram's friend won't either. Now on to the next quest. Dillon got up from his chair and excused himself.

Matt Hastings' wife was coming out of the Roslyn food store in Roslyn, Washington. Three miles from Cle Elum. Her cart was filled with groceries. As she was putting the bags into her car one of them broke loose and the vegetables spilled all over the back seat.

"Ma'am, may I help you?" Dillon Russell said, as he got out of his car. The car had no license plates on it.

Cindy turned around with a bunch of celery in her hands. "Oh, no thank you. I wasn't paying attention, that's all. I was thinking about the birthday dinner I need to cook for my next door neighbor. There'll be fifteen people showing up."

He grinned, then he knocked the celery out of her hands.

"What are you doing?" Cindy yelled.

"I'm trying to get your attention."

"Well, stop it! And leave me alone. Get away from here."

"Ma'am I need you to come with me."

"What!"

Dillon yanked Cindy toward him. "This way, into my car."

Cindy clawed and scratched her way out of his hold. She started to run, but Dillon grabbed her again. This time he slapped her in the face and briskly turned her around. He took a small rope and tied her hands.

HELP! HELP!" Cindy yelled long and loud. She struggled, trying to pull her arms loose. What does this maniac want? This can't be happening. Not here. Not now. What was this man going to do to her? Her children, she needed them. God! God! She needed help!

People in front of the grocery store looked at both of them.

Dillon finished tying her hands. Some men started running toward them. Quickly Dillon pushed her into his car, got in, and drove away.

"Stop this. Please," Cindy yelled. "What do you want? Who are you?"

"No sex. Don't worry. And will you stop crying?"

Cindy moved up from the back seat and started knocking Dillon with her head. He turned and slapped her face. Then he drove off to the side of the road, jumped out, opened the back door, and hit Cindy straight in the face. He hit her again in the eyes. She fell backwards. She was unconscious.

Dillon looked around to be sure there were no cars stopping. He drove away to a rented cabin off of Pease Road. At the cabin he chained her to a bed, checked to be sure she couldn't escape, and that the masking tape on her mouth was tightly secured. Her clothes were left on. He pulled out his cell phone, snapped a picture, and drove away to meet two associates. After a brief talk, both cars drove off to Matt's farm in Cle Elum.

Matt was working hard by the side of the barn with one of his sons when Dillon got out of his car. "Afternoon, Matt."

Matt rolled his eyebrows. "Do I know you?"

Dillon laughed. "In a roundabout way. I'm Dillon Russell."

At first Matt wasn't sure who that was, then it clicked. He asked his son to go inside and warm up the cheese sauce, and get the kitchen ready for Cindy. Matt turned back to Dillon. "Well, Mr. Russell, I was wondering if I'd ever see you face to face. Hiram told me you might finally back off on my property, and drop your idea of an irrigation system to satisfy mainly your needs—not the needs of the family farmers surrounding this region. Are you here to finally apologize?"

"The reason I'm here is to smarten you up. I've offered you some money way over your current value. Are you going to keep being insolent and somewhat foolish?"

"What you keep forgetting is that this is a rural community and we don't want your development. You're not going to erode away this turf. We country bumpkins don't ever intend to move. Our work is connected to our lives. We grew up here; we are nurtured by the spirit of this country. My wife and my sons call this home. We're happy right here no matter what the drain is on our money."

"There's a shortage of housing that's occurring in this area Matt, and developing new homes is much more agreeable to the government than family farmers stuck with very little funds. Money runs this world, no matter how idealistic you are."

"You're insane. This area is not in any turmoil, nor are the farmers. There's some uncertainties, sure; but no flood of trouble. We work the land with compassion and devotion. Get out of here. I've got to finish the barn and get ready for Cindy. We have farmers coming over for dinner."

"Matt, take my offer before I steamroll through your land. I need your farm, and I'll get it. No matter how unwise you think I am, you can not last long here. Oh, and I doubt if your wife will join your grassy group for dinner tonight. She's a little tied up with other things." Dillon tilted his cell phone toward Matt to look at a photo.

Matt grabbed Dillon's shirt.

"Matt, you can tear me to pieces, and you can never give up your farm for a bundle of money, but you'll never get your wife back unless you stop your antics and take my offer, and live a clean life with your wife."

Matt let go of Dillon. Cindy was his golden treasure. Her love was deep. She cared endlessly for him, and for the family. Yes, of course, she had worries about their money. Yes, she was concerned for her children's welfare. But she believed in Matt. She believed in this farm, and the beauty it radiates outward and into their bodies. It was nature bound in stillness and peace, as she always said. What if he lost her? He wouldn't be able to continue; he'd go nuts. She was the added passion to keep this farm alive. "When can I talk to Cindy?"

"When you sign the contract." Dillon pulled out some papers and gave them to Matt.

"I'll sign once Cindy is here. And she needs to be here in an hour. Am I clear? I don't trust you at all."

"That makes us even. I don't trust you, Matt. When you sign this paper, then she will be delivered. If you don't sign, you'll never see her again. I doubt if you—"

Matt pulled Dillon toward him, kneed him in the groin, and threw him to the ground, ready to stomp on his face; but just then a gun was fired in the air. Matt quickly turned. Two men got out of the other car, pointing their guns at Matt. One of them started lifting Dillon up and into the back seat of his car. The other man got into the second car. Before he left, he threw out Cindy's wedding ring. Then, they drove away grinning like a weird wolfs.

Matt picked up her ring and held it in his fist. Stunned, he turned and walked back to the house. His young sons came running toward him, filled with fear. Damn it! What would his children do without this farm, without their mother? His sons grabbed him hard. He grabbed back even harder.

CHAPTER 13

The wind was blowing wild all along the Seattle waterfront. Gage looked out the hallway window of The Inn as he was walking toward Hiram's office. Most of the sailboats in the marina already had their sails stripped and extra lines had been added to most of the boats. The waves were hitting the marina with full force, splashing violently onto the docks. Thank the gods we put tall pilings on the floating docks a month ago. How in the hell did Hiram know it was time to do that? This evening's weather wasn't even forecasted.

He walked into Hiram's office. Hiram was in a chair reviewing some papers. "This whole calamity is turning into a kiss of death," Gage said. "Matt's fallin' apart. More threats are being thrown at him. He doesn't know what to do. I don't know what to do."

Hiram waved his hand toward the couch next to the window. "Easy up, ace buddy. We all have times of doubts and difficulties. You sure ain't alone. What's goin' on, Gage?"

"Matt just called me. Dillon has kidnapped his wife and is demanding that he sign his farm over to him or Matt will never see Cindy again? I thought we had stopped him from these threats? How's this happening? And—we still haven't a clue what to do with Brice's demand to hand over The Inn to him."

Hiram shook his head a little.

"Fuck it! Never mind," Gage said. "I got to handle this instead of always running to THE MAN." Gage got up from the couch, kicked himself, and started to leave.

Hiram threw his coffee cup against the door. The coffee splashed all over Gage's face. Hiram pulled him back, kicked the pieces of the cup, and threw Gage onto the couch. "Shit happens. So what! You face the fear, whatever the fear is, but don't judge it. Don't even grab at it. Ya just feel it, really feel it, and breathe deeply. Then let it go. Close your eyes, as you're doing it." He placed Gage's hand on his stomach. "Keep at it, five minutes."

Gage kept his damn hand on his belly. The Inn? Was he going to lose it to Brice? Would he really lose his treasure? And Matt? His farm is also tumbling apart. Why in—stop it you blockhead! Just keep breathing.

After the five minutes Hiram turned away from the window. "Gage, you can pause for a while. And, you're lookin' better. Good going. And yes, we're in another kettle of hot water. You've already told me about Brice and the notice to hand over The Inn. And now there's a tornado heading toward Matt. Dillon's firing up the pressure to take over Matt's land. I'll check with Tony on this. Speaking of which: Tony's come up with an idea for the Brice difficulty."

Hiram poured another coffee. "Wonder if we create two demonstrations happening at the same time. This would take place just a little South of The Inn's waterfront. One would be praising Chief Seattle's history. Then in a few moments another set of demonstrators would come from behind the first group and criticize Chief Seattle, and praise Chief Leschi. Then the first group will start criticizing Leschi. They'll bring up Chief Leschi's history in a distorted way, making it sound as though he was rotten, shady, and deserved to be hung. All this will hit the news. Brice will know it has something to do with us, because it'll be staged close to our property. He'll want to get back at us. Brice will lose his cool. Which means he'll start to take some action, but the actions will be somewhat impetuous, below par, giving us room to intervene. We just might have room to bust in and bag him. "

"You really think so?"

"Don't act like a babe in the woods. Sure, it's a good idea. But nothing in this shit-ass-world is certain or constant. We'll do our best actions, but don't attach your thirty-three or thirty-five on them."

"My 'thirty' what?"

"Forget it, it's prison talk for 'high hopes'. Just remember, don't ever attach to expectations, and ya'll always have a feelin' of soft soap inside yourself: a feeling of peace and ease. Right now get over to Matt's and calm him down. You said that he said some of Dillon's men have surrounded the farm. I'll make sure Tony will have some of his men jump over here and go with you to Matt's. When you're back we'll talk about the demise of Dillon."

Gage walked back to his suite and started looking at his schedule. He needed to be sure if today was good to get over to Matt's farm. As he was checking the stats, Simmons came out of the bedroom and into the suite's living room. She walked over and stroked Gage's cheek. "I've had another great sleep. This hotel is an ideal place to recoup."

"You look a hundred percent better, Simmons. And, I'm glad you love the place."

"Absolutely. But now that I'm taking a closer look, you're not so cheery looking. Has the stormy weather outside got you worried?"

"I wish it was just the weather. There are different storms coming from different directions surrounding Matt. You gave your courage and heart to try and help Matt get free from Dillon's fury. However, Dillon's back with more madness. He's kidnapped Matt's wife. Matt has to give up his farm or his wife is dead. Violence is ready to erupt. I've got to get over there and calm him down for the moment, until Hiram and I figure out a way to stop Dillon."

"Gage, don't be foolish. You can't go over there. Yes, it's good to care about someone, but you can't over-care, you can't get blinded and lose sight of you safety."

"Simmons, you went over to get information from Dillon so we could help Matt. And you did it knowing that Dillon was a dangerous person."

"Of course, I wanted to help Matt, but it was Hiram that sprang the spring to get me involved. As Hiram said, I looked liked Dillon's wife, who he worshiped before and after she died. While I was captured, I heard Dillon's men are eagle-eyeing Matt's place from time to time. You'd get trapped by Dillon's men."

"There's just no option. I've got to help him."

"Help him, yes. But get Hiram to go. Or, one of Hiram's hulky friends."

Gage held her hand. "Hiram has the guts of a gator, but I can't have him harmed. He's my friend, or rather, he's our friend.

Simmons threw herself onto Gage. "Gage, I don't want you hurt. I need you. I want to live life with you. Please, call someone else."

"Simmons, my life is tied to several things: you, Hiram, and The Inn. Here you are protected, and you love The Inn. Hiram works like hell to always protect The Inn. And right now, Matt needs to be protected. I've got to give him some confidence and courage that we'll find a way to get him out of the can of worms he's in."

"Why can't Matt come over here while all the mayhem is going on."

"He can't. He has to work the farm. And even if he had the money for a farm manager, he wouldn't leave for fear of what Dillon's men might do to the farm."

"Gage, everyone has pressures in this world. You can't be a stupid Boy Scout and try and save them all, especially Matt. You've got to become realistic right now."

"There's no one else stepping in and helping Matt out of the trouble. You tried, and almost got killed. I have to try."

"Yes, *almost got killed*. Gage, Dillon and his men don't care about anything except to achieve their goal. If you get in the way, you'd be like a mosquito to them: you'll be irritating, worthless, and deserved to be killed. Stop this. Have Hiram find help."

Gage shook his head and heart. "Tony tried putting a stop to Matt's troubles several days ago. Obviously something didn't go right. So Hiram is now finding a new way to throw a different block into Dillon's greed. He's doing his best; we all are. But right now you need to remember who Matt is. He needs his wife back from Dillon's ropes and chains. She fills him with hope and confidence, especially when he loses his balance in life. I have to go to him. Not someone else. I have to go and help him."

Simmons started crying.

Gage softly held her chin in his hand and turned her head toward him. "For us—for you and me Simmons—love isn't just a feeling or a fantasy, it's a bridge that binds us and will never be taken away. I love you Simmons. Always will."

CHAPTER 14

Gage hit the car's horn as he drove up to the front of Matt's farm house. Matt turned around from the side of the barn as Gage got out. Matt waved and started coming to him. Tony's three muscle men who traveled with Gage stayed in their car behind the trees. Matt walked over to Gage and gave him one hell of a bear hug. "My God Gage, you're here. Right here. Come on, let's get up to the porch."

"Matt, I didn't think you needed some soft words over the phone. You need someone you can see and touch." Gage turned and gave Matt a similar bear hug.

"Gage, as I told you, she was stolen from me. I'm burning with pain inside, and it won't go away. Without her in my arms, I feel like life is a cold oven. My whole dream for this farm is over." Matt started mumbling. "I—I need Cindy back, I have to have her back." He grabbed Gage's hand as he brushed some tears away.

Gage was stuck in a muddy rut. He had left Simmons singing the blues as he came to support Matt. And now Matt was singing them, too. He had to help him out of this gutter of grief. He would take—

Several gunshots were fired in the air. Gage quickly straightened up. Tony's men had gotten out of their car and were shooting toward the top of the barn where some men with binoculars were watching Gage and Matt. One of the men on the roof started to fire back but was shot in the shoulder. He rolled off the roof.

Matt's children ran out of the house, yelling as they came to their dad. "Daddy. Daddy." Matt grabbed them and lifted them onto his lap, kissing them lovingly. "It's OK. It's OK. Some of Gage's men have stopped those stupid gate-crashers."

Orin, the head of Tony's men, ran behind the barn with his men. Moments later they came back to the car with the wounded man and two other guys. Gage, Matt, and the boys also went to the car.

"Listen up you jerk," Orin said to the injured man, "if you want to jet to a hospital, you'd better tell us why you're here." Orin turned to Matt. "Better take the kids back to the house, this could get rough."

Matt shook his head in utter confusion. "Gage, come on back with us."

"Matt, I need to stay here and help with extracting some information from these guys. I'll join you when we get info on Dillon or Cindy. But right now, why don't you go to the porch."

As Matt was walking away Orin smashed the wounded man in the face. "Why the hell are you guys here?"

The man mumbled and stuttered for a moment. Another one of the captured men yelled out, "Stop this you dipshit! You do any more of this and Matt's wife is dead meat. Now let us go."

Orin walked over and hit this man in the face too. Then he pointed his gun at the man. "You got thirty seconds. Why the hell are you here?"

There was a short pause. The man kept wiping his face with the cuff of his shirt. "That Matt character was given a timeline to hand over the deed to his farm. We were sent to make sure he didn't talk to any police or outsiders, face to face, till his deadline was due. If he did solicit someone, his wife would be beaten and set up for an even faster ransom. You're the only group we've seen so far."

Gage stepped forth. "Looks like you can become dead meat in a few seconds unless you start helping us further. Is Dillon in Spokane now?"

"We have no idea, We're—"

"Oh, shut up." Gage turned to Orin and motioned him to come to the large tree by the car. "Orin, I'd like to take these men back to The Inn and have a gutsy guy called Hiram talk with them. He's a pro at abstracting information. Will the wounded man be able to go with us?"

"Yeah, he only has shoulder wounds. His main pain is from rattling off the roof. I'll find out where their car is and we'll stuff them in it. Then we'll all follow you to your hotel."

Gage went back to Matt. His two sons were sitting on his lap as he was biting down hard on his lower lip. "I'm going to take those men back to The Inn," Gage said, "and have Hiram apply what he learned in prison: to be hard-hitting persuasive." He put his hands around the small children. "We'll find out where Cindy is Matt, don't worry. We'll get her back to you so you can love her forever."

Matt nodded while more tears started to flow.

The little boys looked at their father.

Gage looked at their father. He'd do anything to help this farm-family man so his tears would take a powder and his eyes would shine like sunlight.

As the men were getting into different cars, Gage called Hiram on his cell phone. "Well, it's been an adventure." Gage told Hiram the whole story of the scene with Dillon's men on the barn roof, and that Gage and Tony's men were going to bring them back to The Inn so Hiram could 'interview' them.

It took over an hour. When they arrived at The Inn, Hiram and Dale Davenport, head of Security, met them at the hotel's entrance. They took the back elevator up to Hiram's suite. "Orin," Hiram said, "what's the injured man's name?"

"Ryan."

Hiram walked on over to the man. "Well Ryan, looks like you had a fall from heaven. You'll need to get that shoulder fixed soon. I'm sure Dillon will make arrangements for you. Speaking of which, I need to toss you a question you've been asked before, but you're in a gentler environment now, so it should go well. Where's Dillon? He's not spending time in The Financial Center in Spokane. We've checked. Where is he now, and what's his house address?"

The man didn't answer.

"I doubt if you want to irritate me."

"This is going around in circles. If you want Dillon, let me talk to him first on the phone."

"I don't make compromises, dude. Right now is the time to act. Where's Dillon?"

"I can't give out—"

Hiram grabbed the man's shirt, almost tearing it off the guy, and walked to the window with him. "Instead of pissing me off, answer the question: where is he?"

"Stop acting like a fool. Let me call him now."

Hiram crashed open the wide window and hauled the man into the air. "Answer my question or you're out the window, and you'll be dead meat as you drop to your death. Answer now!"

The man flailed his hands in the air and slapped Hiram. "You son of a bitch!"

Hiram hit him in the face and tossed him out the window. All the men's faces flashed with surprise. Gage dropped his mouth wide open. "Hiram! Jesus Christ, you can't do this. We can't have—"

"You!" Hiram pointed to another man on the couch. "You want a ride to hell? Where's Dillon?"

"Goddamn you, will you slow down," the man yelled out.

Hiram jacked the man off the couch, lifted him up, and walked toward the wide window. "Hold it! Stop! He's somewhere in Spokane."

"I know that. I wanna know exactly where! He's not at his normal house." Hiram grabbed the man's shirt and opened the window, ready to toss him out.

" OK, OK. South Perry. Living in a condo, around Grant Park."

" Specifics, shit head." Hiram lifted him up and towards the window

" His condo . . . his condo complex is on Arthur St, called the Park View."

Hiram put the man down. He was white as ghost. Gage wasn't doing too well, either. Hiram walked over to Dale. "Dale, take all these men, along with Tony's muscle men, to a first floor side room; and get that Ryan out of the canvass we set up today on the second floor. Have everyone wait for me. I'll call Tony D and have him arrange to put these three guys in some secure place." Dale nodded.

Hiram looked over to Gage who didn't seem too stable.

Gage was next to the window. He was either going to faint or throw up. "Hiram, how did you know to put a damn canvas below here so anyone you threw out the window wouldn't be smashed to death on the walkway?"

"Gage, when you called earlier telling me you were at Matt's farm, and you were on the way over here with some of Dillon's men, I thought this little window escapade would get one of these guys to open up quickly."

Gage was brushing his brow. "Hiram, you're not just a genius, you're a mental giant."

"Skip the fuzzy words. Right now we've got to get some of our staff and teach them how to become demonstrators on the streets so good ol' Brice Hafer will hear their story."

CHAPTER 15

Ten demonstrators walked onto the pedestrian overpass just south of The Inn. Below them Alaskan Way was busy with traffic. They took out large American flags, colorful banners, and signs that had two different messages. The first couple of banners read: Chief Leschi was unfair. The other banners read: Chief Seattle was the best. The demonstrators waved the flags and beat their drums, yelling: 'God bless Chief Seattle. He gave us hope. He had passion and fire in his belly. This city wouldn't be here without him. Chief Leschi was not even close to the goals and gifts of Chief Seattle. He was full of pride and arrogance. He deserved to be murdered by the government!'

Cars below the overpass started honking their horns. A crowd of bystanders on the waterfront were staring up at the demonstrators.

All of a sudden another group of demonstrators come onto the pedestrian overpass from the other side. They threw plastic balls filled with red dye at the Chief Seattle demonstrators. Quickly they held up several different signs that read: Chief Seattle was a jelly-fish. He tried to be strong, but he wasn't. Chief Seattle submitted to the power of the white men. Chief Leschi didn't! Chief Leschi was genuine. He wanted the rights given back to all Native Americans.

More red dye was thrown.

The Chief Seattle demonstrators came running toward the Leschi group. They hit the Leschi group with their signs, and started kicking and punching. The Leschi group struck back. But more Chief Seattle people came running up the ramp and began fighting. They threw the Leschi banners over the railing, and started tearing off the clothes of the Leschi demonstrators. Most of that group were naked as they bolted away.

This was all aired live on KIRO-TV.

Brice Hafer threw the remote control at the television, cracking the flat screen. What the hell was going on? This was no celebration for either of the Indian chiefs. And why was the Leschi group ridiculed and jammed off the damn bridge? Chief Leschi was a leader. A solid leader. Not like fuckin' Chief Seattle. Leschi pushed hard for fairness and honor. And what did he get—death! He was executed by the fuckin' state government. The white leaders didn't want to give up the land they had already taken from the Redskins, so they hanged him to shut him up. Brice started sniffling and shivering. He couldn't let this stand as it is. People have to know, they're going to know the difference between a weakling and a warrior!

He got on the phone and called Mark Schmit, the man who had installed the boombox at The Inn almost a week ago, causing all sorts of trauma for Gage McClure. "Mark, come on over here in an hour. We're going to do some planning on how to detonate The Inn at the Pier, and how to blow up the rest of the goddamn waterfront. Then we're gonna figure a way to loud-speaker all of Seattle about their hollow history. How Chief Seattle caused the damn Yakima Indian War, and why the hell Chief Seattle ever signed the insane Treaty of Point Elliott."

The next day at three in the morning. some of Brice's men were on a silent electric boat on the south side of The Inn at the Pier, slowly traveling along The Inn's thick pier foundations. They had some C-4s, blasting caps, and a bunch of TNT in the bow of the boat. At a designated spot they stopped. Two men in diving suits put on their scuba tanks, grabbed the boxes of TNT, and—a flood of lights got triggered.

The men in the boat stopped, looked upward.

Shots were fired around the boat, and from under the pier a speaker screeched out the command to turn off the engine and raise their hands. "If you don't start raising your hands in two seconds we start firing the guns at you." Everyone in the boat raised their hands. "Now, you, the guy at the stern, move your boat over to the large pillar in front of you where there's a rope ladder. You other guys keep your hands raised." Everyone obeyed.

As the boat came to the piling, Hiram came down the ladder and got in the boat, holding a 44 Magnum in his hand. "OK, move back out to Elliott Bay, and then to the marina at the north side of The Inn."

When the boat docked, Gage met them along with a couple other men. After some quick talk with Hiram, the security men escorted the three captives into a storage room at the back of the hotel. The TNT and C-4s were also carried into the storage room.

Down in the room, Hiram finally introduced himself to the three tided up men. "I can see you boys didn't come by to drop into the hotel's cocktail lounge for some jazz. And, it's obvious Brice Hafer didn't come along with you." Hiram pulled out his 44. "When the cops come and see the three of you dead, it will be obvious that we were defending The Inn against your attempt to hurt The Inn. So, it's not sweat off my back it you don't answer my question, I'll simply kill ya. We'll start with you." He pointed to one of the guys in a scuba gear. "What's Brice's home phone?"

Instead of answering, the man sweated like a wet hog. "No answer?" Hiram shot the man in the legs and arms.

Gage's eyes were stinging. What was Hiram doing? You can't shoot a person. You can't! "Hiram, stop this."

"Shut up Gage."

Hiram turned to other guy with scuba gear. "What's his telephone number?"

"What are you, only a clod with muscles, no brains? Get the—"

"Shut the fuck up. What's his number?" The man didn't answer.

Hiram started to shoot, but the man yelled, "Damn you! All right, I'll give it to ya."

"OK, shout it out. And throw us your cell phone. Gage, take down the number."

The scuba guy gave out the number.

"Gage, call Brice on his cell. We need to see him."

Brice's phone rang; he picked up. "Mark, are the bombs placed in sequence, with the caps ready to be detonated?"

"This isn't Mark. Brice, you actually think you'd get away with your craziness. Get over here and turn yourself in, now!"

"Who's this?"

"Gage McClure. And if you don't get over here, we'll turn your men in. They'll be interrogated. Your whole life will be in shambles."

"I doubt that you'll—"

Dale Davenport ran into the storage room. "Gage, Hiram, we've got more trouble. On the west side of the pier, underneath the pier, there's more covered bombs encased in thick boulders. And they've got classified timers. The timers are ticking. They could go off any time. "

Gage yelled into the phone. "Brice, what the hell's going on? There are more explosives."

"Your place will explode this morning. Now release my men and get them on a taxi. A taxi, not any of your fucking hotel cars. Are we clear? Have someone keep looking at the timers to notice if the timers are off or on. I'll turn them off now. But if the taxi doesn't reach a specific destination in thirty minutes, the timers will go on and stay on. My men know where a taxi should take them. Thirty minutes, McClure. Starting now."

Gage squeezed his hand hard. If The Inn was blown apart, there'd be no reason to go on. He was nothing without his walls of wonder. He'd lose—calm down. If you'd remember Hiram's wisdom you'd actually see that life isn't that solid and secure. It's full of change. So do some belly breathing, and flow with change, at least a little.

Gage took in some air, then got back on the phone. "Your threat is dramatic, but definitely not solid. Brice, sure, you can hit the timers and this hotel will blow apart. But then we'll just start to build a new one. You'll be captured and jailed, probably for life, because your men will be interrogated intensely by the police."

"Sharp, McClure, but not that sharp. I don't give a shit if you rebuild. The only thing I want is to blow up all of the Seattle waterfront, and then have Chief Leschi praised for his real truth. I'll have all that done before any cop can catch me or my team of arsonists." Brice hung up.

Gage turned and looked for Hiram. He wasn't here.

"He's outside on the pier, on the seventh pillar," one of the security guards said. "Come on, I'm supposed to take you there."

They met Hiram and several of the maintenance men at the end of the pier. There were swing ladders, tools, portable lights, and canisters all over the place. Hiram walked over to Gage. "As soon as Dale yelled out that there were more bombs with timers tickin' away, it didn't take an idiot to realize we had to stop the timers, no matter what Brice was saying to you on the phone. The guy can't be trusted. After I took a look at the bombs and boulders, I ran with several men to the maintenance room. We picked up plenty of liquid nitrogen that we use to freeze water and oil pipes on the pier, and one of our high-speed drills." Hiram pointed to the flood light that was turned on under the pier. "As you can see, we're almost done. We've drenched the timers with the liquid nitrogen. They're frozen now, and they've stopped their threat."

"Hiram, you've done the magic again. Who are you? Brice was going to blast us apart. But you've re-arranged his detonations so we're safe! By the stars, when I die, may I meet you in Vanuatu?"

"Where the hell's that?"

"Never mind, it's in the South Pacific; it's beautiful. Nude women walk the streets. All right, back to basics: how do we protect The Inn against any more of Brice's madness?"

"I've already thought of that. We'll put flood lights under the pier and the whole length of the pier. We'll also put up more surveillance cameras under the pier to coordinate with the flood lights. And we'll take four of our boats out of the marina and have security staff them at night, seven days a week, for at least four months."

Gage hit his chest, then hugged Hiram, and kissed him on the cheek.

Hiram broke loose. "Damn the Gods! Stop that kissin' shit."

"Hiram, who the hell are you? How do you come up with all these gem stones so soon? Was it fate we met in that restaurant where you were about to slam your fist into the owners face?"

"The law of karma, Gage. Karma floods this land and affects every aspect of our lives. OK, skip this Zen stuff. You jump up and get some sleep. I'll finish here with the boys, then tie Brice's men up before I send them to the cops this morning. Doubt if Brice can now do any more surprises to the hotel. And, Tony D has gotten back as to why Dillon has not stopped going after Matt's land. Somehow he's gotten rid of any evidence with the Cook Islands Trust. I'm gonna talk with Anna about going to Spokane again. We need to get the name of the WSDA agent Dillon is bribing and have that man get nailed. Dillon's son is somewhat taken by Anna. We can use that to our advantage."

CHAPTER 16

After Hiram got a bit of rest he walked into the manager's office. Anna was looking over a Shift Audit Report, working like a demon to analyze all the details. Gage was right on course to train her to become a manager. She had the mixture of beauty and ability. "Anna, you're working harder than a hooker on Aurora Avenue."

"Na, just tryin' to learn the biz. What's up scoop dog?"

"How's about you and me jet back to Spokane and have Aaron help us out? Matt's in even more trouble now that his wife's been kidnapped by Dillon. And his farm's gonna be taken away unless we can get some info on the state official that allows Dillon to cut political corners."

"I thought you put all the pressure on Dillon already? That's why you already went to Spokane."

"I did, and it should have worked, but it backfired. We have to find the name of the character Dillon is bribing. We need that man's name and number on a business card or in some damn computer file. That's where you come in. When we get to Spokane, I need you to meet up with Aaron again. He seemed attracted to you. If that's true, and if he seems open, ask him if he could lend a hand."

"Christ, one headache after another. Does Gage know about this?"

"Of course."

"So, how do I meet up with Aaron?"

"Remember the cafe in The Bank of America Financial Center? That's where you met him. It could be a favorite hang-out for him during the business day. You may want to give that place another try. If you get to see him, you want to be upfront, sweet, and kind. You need his help. If the conversation is open, get with him after work, and bring him back to the hotel that you and I will be staying at."

"Hiram, why are we gettin' into this again?"

"To pull Matt out of a hole."

"Damn it, we don't even know the dude."

"No, but we know Gage. What am I, an Einstein that has to keep repeating the keys of life to you? We honor Gage for what he did for us, and what he does for others. He's a living soul that reaches into the hearts of hurts, and helps people weather the sting of life. I wouldn't be here if Gage hadn't reached out to me. You wouldn't be here—you wouldn't be alive—if he hadn't reached out to you. Know whada mean?"

Anna paused, looked out the window to the soft waters of Elliot Bay, then turned back to Hiram. "OK, we're off into the wild blue yonder again."

After they landed in Spokane, they checked into the Davenport Hotel. Hiram slept like a log. Anna was restless all night. She sure wasn't going to let herself be captured by Aaron's dad like Simmons was. Hell, living life can be a messy mud pool that's as hard as quicksand to get out of at times. Couldn't her damn world be a little more normal? Couldn't she be a little more confident in playing the chess-game of life? Did she always have to please people and seek approval? Why, why, couldn't she have learned early in life that it was worthless to carry around an empty heart, and a head full of wounds and fog from the past? She bumped with these bubbles most of the night.

In the morning they both had breakfast, walked around the area, then Hiram wished her luck as she got into a cab for the Financial Center.

Once inside the Financial Center she went to the mall's coffee shop and ordered a mocha latte to go. Slowly she walked around the small mall, sipping the coffee and looking at the windows of different stores. She even went into some of the high-class stores. Cocktail dresses with jewel necklines, black blazers, leopard print scarves, and some stiletto sandals, all with high price tags. The gals in the upstairs offices must be pulling in some good pay checks to afford clothes like these. She wasn't making close to—

"Anna," Aaron said out loud. "Anna, what are you doing here?"

"Sipping latte, and trying to decide how women can afford these clothes." She pointed to the last store she was in.

Aaron smiled. "I was just coming to get a coffee too. Come with me while I get cappuccino, and then we can go up to the office and look out the window toward Riverside Park. And don't worry, my dad is not here. It'll be fresh and fun."

They brought their coffees up to the 18th floor. Aaron pushed two chairs over to the window in his office. The sweeping view of Riverside Park was deadly and delicious. "Good God, Aaron, you've got one amazing view. No matter how much your dad grumbles and pushes, you can always come here and be at peace."

"Wish it was that simple; but when he's not here, I do relax. Now, downstairs while I was getting coffee, you said you'd like my help. For what?"

"I sure could use your character and courage, Aaron. As you know the last time I was here with Hiram we tried to have your dad stop his activities with Matt Hastings and his farm. Hiram pulled out some tight pressure. Your dad said he'd stop his antics, but he didn't. In fact he's tightened the hanging knot on Matt. He's kidnapped Matt's wife and is forcing Matt to hand over his farm."

"Anna, I never heard of this. Yes, I know dad wants that farm, and other farms, to expand that whole area and increase his profits. I know he's tried hard, but never have I gotten an idea that he's kidnapped someone's wife."

"We need to help Matt," Anna said. "And, there is a way. One of your dad's love affairs is the ability to bribe government officials to get what he wants. Hiram wants to find this WSDA man who helps your dad push past the limits for extra profit. We sent a lady friend of ours to try and get that info, but she failed and your dad really put her in hell until Hiram forced your dad to let her go."

Aaron's face started to lose color.

"Aaron, you're not looking too sharp. Is this all news to you?"

"You know dad and I have issues on how to communicate. He's never told me about this."

"Aaron, would you come over to the Davenport Hotel with me and meet the Zen guy again, and try and help him find this WSDA agent your dad keeps bribing?"

"Let's go. I can put off my work schedule for a while."

"All right." Anna kissed Aaron on the cheek. Oops, Aaron blushed.

Anna and Aaron walked into a corner room suite at the Davenport Hotel. As they came in, Hiram turned and gave Aaron a slap on the shoulder. "It's mighty good to see you Aaron. Come on, let's go over to the chairs."

"I've told Aaron why we're here and why we need him," Anna said.

"The truth of the matter Aaron, Matt Hastings is a good man with good will. And he's close to losing his wife. His woman cares for the children, works on the farm, and comforts Matt during his long hours in the fields. I tried a very savvy approach with your father to stop all this nonsense. It should have worked, but your father found a way to get around it. As Anna probably told you, what I need now is the name of the state official that your father is bribing. I also found out that your father hasn't been in his office for a while. And he doesn't stay in his beautiful house; he's in a condo on Park View. He obviously is waiting in the background and staying out of harms way, until the pressure on Matt will be effective."

"Jesus Christ, Hiram, you've got more facts than I do. All my dad said to me was that he needed massive quietude and no disturbance till the project he's working on is finished. He gave me a month of paper work, and if anyone needed him I'd have to contact dad's secretary."

Hiram shook his head. "I had a woman try and cuddle up with your father so he would take her to his mansion. He did, and she found the name and number of the WSDA agent. But your dad caught her and bonded her till I forced him to let her go. We still don't have the name of the guy. Can you take us back to his office so we can double search it? "

"It would be pretty hard to let you come into the office during the day. No one's allowed in his office. But Anna and I can go to dad's house and search his home-office. He does most of his private work there. You couldn't come because the security there would stop you and probably call dad. You look too tough. However Anna can act as my girlfriend. I'll tell them I just want to show her the house that may one day belong to me. We'll go inside the house, look around, then go inside the office, and ramble through his files and business card holders. We can go now."

"Great, do it. But Aaron, be careful. Nothing can happen to Anna."

They arrived at Dillon's estate. As they went through the gates, Anna kept looking at the forest and hills. This place was breathtaking. They got out of the car and walked to the front door. Aaron opened the door with his key. As they started to walk into the hallway, a butler came up to them. "Aaron, I haven't seen you for ages. You look good. How's life treating you, my boy?"

"Life is good. Working hard in the company. I'm taking a small break right now so I can show my girlfriend the house that will probably be passed on to me."

"And what's the ladies name?"

Anna stuck out her hand to shake the butler's hand. "I'm Kathy Myers. I'm Aaron's girlfriend. And it's good to not just meet you, but to see this wonderful place."

"Colin," Aaron said, "I wanted to show Kathy around the house, and to see the view from the back. We'll only be here an hour; I have much work to finish up at the office."

Anna smiled.

"Aaron, usually your father lets me know if you're coming. But . . . well . . . I guess it's OK. You'll only be here for a while. Nice to have met you ma'am."

Anna nicely nodded as she and Aaron walked into the living room with a huge fire place and gigantic views of the rolling hills and forest. They crossed the room and stepped into an office with some desks and a large curved sofa circling around a gas fireplace made of different stones. The front wall was all glass, with more views of the forest and mountains on the horizon. "This is dad's big office. There's another smaller office on the top floor. But, first, let's see if we can find anything in this room."

They both searched for a while but found nothing, so they left and went up a set of stairs with some stunning curvatures. The steps were made out of bright cherry wood to give off some kind of floating effect, and the curved walls were made of sandstone, or hell, it could be limestone, or granite. Anna didn't know, and it didn't matter because the whole staircase was like a surrealistic painting, and the lights on the walls made the stones sparkle with colors of gold, white, and blue. Incredible.

Anna and Aaron went into the small office. Aaron went over to the desk and turned on the computer, inserted the security code, and started looking through files and folders for any link to the WSDA. Anna opened several drawers looking for business cards.

"Anna, come here. I think I've found it."

Anna looked to where the cursor was pointing. "Aaron, you genius."

Aaron quickly emailed the states on the card to one of his unnamed accounts.

While they were at the computer, Dillon Russell burst into the room with a bodyguard. "Aaron, I was surprised to hear you were here at the estate. And I'm doubly surprised to see that this girl is your girlfriend. Get real! She works for a man called Hiram Smith, who is trying to interfere with my acquisitions and assets. He's a sentimental sap who thinks his heart is the highway to practicality. A little like you Aaron." Dillon walked over to the computer and looked at the screen. "Well Aaron, you've got Zak Nebard's name and number. You've never wanted his information before. It couldn't be because of your 'girlfriend,' could it? "

"Dad, give a look at your emails and see what was sent just before you burst in here."

Dillon quickly looked at the screen. The email was sent to some AOL account. "What the shit did you do, you little grasshopper? Who did you send that to?"

"Just doing what you do dad, backing things up when I can."

"Who's AOL address is this?"

"If I told you you'd go berserk, and probably have your muscle man slap me all around the room. What you can do is realize that right now you're in some thick molasses. And you'd better let us leave, or who gets that email will pull your ass into jail."

Aaron got up from the chair and walked to Anna.

"Hold it, you asshole! What are you doing? Trying to ruin my company? Tell me who you sent that to."

"You double idiot. I'll answer all you questions after you let us go. If you don't let us leave now, in one hour you're going to be in a pile of shivers and shit. Your whole career will be blasted apart. And dear dad, you'll end up in prison. Sure, you've been a mean father but I'm not trying to get any payback, all I want to do right now is to protect Anna from your anger. Let us leave this place. In two hours I'll be back in the downtown office. We can talk there. OK?"

"Clyde, handcuff Anna," Dillon ordered the bodyguard.

The guard pushed Aaron out of the way and started to nail Anna. Only thing was, Anna wasn't a normal woman. She immediately kicked the guy in the balls. The guard yelled loudly. Then she ran toward the door. Dillon grabbed her hair, but she did a side-turn and jabbed a finger straight into his eye. He bent over, screaming like a red fox. She quickly opened the door; she was almost free. But the damn guard caught her and cuffed her.

"All right Aaron," Dillon said. "Game time is over,"

"Clyde, rip her blouse off and start slapping her."

The bodyguard obeyed. Anna started screaming.

"Now Aaron, he'll keep doing this until you tell me who you sent that email to."

Anna kept screaming.

"Stop it! Stop it. I sent it to me so I could be sure I'd have it if things got out of hand by your anger and ill temper."

"Well, finally you're getting real. Go to this computer and open up your email at your AOL. Let me see you sent it to you, to be sure."

Aaron did as he was told. In a few moments he showed his father the email. Dillon nodded with acceptance. "Now go with Clyde. He's going to put Anna in a room, and put you in the next room. Of course the doors will be locked."

Dillon went to the small sink and wiped his eye with cold water. Then he sat down, pulled out a personal notebook. Dialed Hiram Smith's cell.

"Hello."

"Ah, Mr. Smith. Dillon Russell here."

"What! Mr. Russell, where are you?"

"May I ask where are you?"

" Skip it. Let's get to the bottom line. Why are you calling?"

"Your little charmer went to my mansion today, along with my son. It's the same mansion dear Simmons went to trying to find the WSDA's name. As you know Simmons was abused severely for making such an attempt. Anna is going to have the same harm done to her, if you make any more attempts to stop me. Why don't you back off completely, and let me finish my business with all the farm lands? Anna and Aaron will be released when this is all over. Get smart." Dillon hung up.

Hiram was going to kill the bastard. Maybe kill himself, too. He took his Smith and Wesson out of his coat pocket. She was a handsome piece of gleaming silver and gunmetal blue, with a tight coil hammer spring and a comfortable grip. He kept looking at it, then put the gun down, and called Gage.

Gage answered. "Hiram, I was getting worried. Did she get the info?"

"Don't know. But what happened was she got caught, along with Aaron. I just got off the phone with Dillon. He said to back off and let him continue with Matt's farm. When it's all over, Anna and Aaron will be released."

"This is absurd. All he does is capture our women. Our chances of helping Matt are getting damn dim. We've got to get Anna back. Shit, look what he did to Simmons."

"Dillon said the same thing, Gage. Sure, Matt's a good guy, but he ain't family. And Dillon is going to pay him some greenbacks for the farm. Maybe we should just ease off on all our efforts. Let Dillon buy him out."

"Can't, and you know it. Matt's a friend. If any friend needs help, we help them. Friendship is more important than money; it's medicine for life; it enriches life."

Hiram paused. "You make good sense, my man. Let's put some elbow grease into all this when I get back." They both hung up.

Gage kept shaking his head. Somehow they'd find a way to rescue Matt. But was he able to protect Anna? Did he have enough brain power? Did he only dream he could accomplish certain goals, but never had the know-how or the top dog talent to do so? Stop this! Pull yourself together. Enough of this poor-me talk.

Simmons walked into the room. Gage looked up. "Gage, you . . . you look like a sick mouse." She came up to him and gave him a kiss along with a gentle hug. "What's happening?"

He clinched his teeth. "As you know, Anna and Hiram went over to Spokane to see Aaron to try and get the damn name of the WSDA agent. Things blew apart. Anna and Aaron are both captured."

"What's going on with this whole fish story?" Simmons said. "When I was in Dillon's mansion, before I was caught, I had found the agent's name on an index card. There were several cards with— wait a sec." She was lost in some sky castle. "WSDA was written on the index card I picked up, along with an agent's name. I can't remember his name. But now that I'm focusing like a witch, there was something that did catch my attention. 'Bionic' was also written on the card. Gage, that could be a code Dillon and the agent use for their hushed money deals. Or, could the agent actually be bionic? Could he have a bionic arm or leg or foot? If he does, it wouldn't take much work to see if there is a bionic person in the WSDA." She turned, smiled wide, and gave Gage a bear hug, as though it was Hug Day. "Why not have Hiram call his magic man about this?"

"Simmons, you're sexy and sharp." He touched her cheek and kissed her eye, then jumped over to the phone. "Hiram, we may finally have a way to pressure Dillon. The WSDA agent Dillon works with might have an odd feature. He may actually have some kind of bionic part attached to him. I'm not joking. If that might be true we can certainly find out who he is and where he is. Can you ask Tony D to use his resources and find out if there is anyone in WSDA headquarters with an artificial body part—an arm, a leg, whatever?"

Gage got off the phone and went back to Simmons. As he began to hug her, he noticed something up in the sky. Two hot air balloons were flying over Pike Place Market. They had flashing lights that formed large wake-up calls. One balloon had the sound of praise for its message: 'Chief Leschi fought for freedom. The greatest chief of all Native Americans.' The other balloon had the message of shame: 'Chief Seattle submitted to Governor Stevens' wants and wishes constantly. He pretended to be heroic, but wasn't.'

The Market was Seattle's most popular tourist destination and the 33rd most visited tourist attraction in the world. Crowds of people were pointing toward the balloon. Suddenly there was an explosion on Pier 69, where the Port of Seattle had its headquarters. Alarms started wailing. Gage and Simmons jerked their heads toward the explosion. Fire was erupting on the back side of the pier. Gage's phone started ringing. He picked up.

"Gage, a Brice Hafer is on the phone. Do you want the call?"

"Yes, transfer the call."

"Mr. McClure, you may have noticed the explosion and the praise for Chief Leschi. As I said, I'm going to demolish the Seattle waterfront and have Washington State pay a price for foolishly damaging Leschi's honor and reputation. Your Inn's set for explosion if you don't follow my advice, and I'll also explode the Bell Harbor Conference Center. So, right now, have the papers for the transfer of your pier signed and delivered by taxi to the address I gave you last week."

"And last week, I told you we need to meet. The Inn's protected, you'll never blast it apart. Get the hell over here now. Talk, generate ideas, create avenues for your dreams that actually work."

"McClure, you're a bastard. I have needs that have to be met. A history that has to be corrected with guts and precision, not with chat and chatter." Brice hung up.

Gage looked out the window. Was his life always filled with pressures? Damn the Gods! No one was stopping this Brice guy. Gage took in a couple of deep breaths, looked at the mountains, looked at Simmons, then quickly dialed a number on his phone. It was to the head administrator of the Nisqually Indian Administration, a Bert Collin.

"Bert Collin, please."

Gage waited a moment. "Yes, Bert Collin here."

"Bert, Gage McClure."

"Good Lord, Gage did you see the balloons, and the explosion on Pier 69?"

"That's why I'm calling you Bert. Last week I gave you a call about Brice Hafer to see if you could help him with his deep need to bring back Chief Leschi's name and honor. Brice is determined to hurt the city of Seattle because of what was done to Chief Leschi in the past. I told him you could help him in a calmer and more creative way to promote the high qualities of Chief Leschi. Well, he never got back to me to take me up on my offer on seeing you. And now—"

"Now he's going wild again. If this Brice character would meet with my staff I think he'll see that there is a good chance that Chief Leschi can be exonerated by a Historical Court. We are already making inroads showing that Leschi was wrongly convicted and executed. I'm sure that Leschi's conviction can be vacated."

"Bert, he's planning to ruin the Seattle waterfront. We've got to find him so he can change course and see that your way is the best way."

"Look, weeks ago there was a conflict between demonstrators for Chief Seattle and Chief Leschi. It ended in confusion and bitterness. How about we set up a demonstration, similar to the last one, but unlike that last thriller —we'll do our demonstration in the air. Each side will point out the positives of the other side's hero, not the negatives. It would be positives swinging back and forth. Of course, Brice probably won't jump for joy at first, but if we organize it right, he could accept some of the complements that would flow between both groups. You could call him later that day. He just might meet with you, and you could bring him over to the Nisqually Administration."

There was a pause on both ends of the phone.

Gage kept looking out toward the majestic, snow capped mountains. Would Brice finally be open to new opportunities? Was gaining a spark of insight, like watching a movie in a theater as you ate popcorn—and then suddenly—you caught on to what was just said on the screen? You jump out of your seat, run out of the theater, and throw your hands in the air for finally understanding what life was about? Life was to be lived, not to be viewed with crushed ideas and judgments.

"And, McClure, we'll also include Native American music during the whole discharge. Tribal music plays an integral role in the daily lives of our Native Americans."

Hiram flew back from Spokane and met Gage in his upstairs office. "It was a mighty neat flight back Gage. Man, I love blue water and clear skies. The info you gave me about the WSDA agent was top-drawer. Tony will get back to me with some feedback on it."

"Glad things are starting to feel good. While you were gone I had a pretty interesting conversation with the guy from the Nisqually Indian Tribe Administration."

"The guy who holds his meetings here now and then?"

"Yup. I called him because Brice Hafer is back to his old tricks again. There were dramatic hot air balloons over The Market promoting Chief Leschi and criticizing Chief Seattle. Many people looked up to the sky. There was also an explosion on the waterfront by Hafer. The Nisqually guy came up with an idea to get Hafer to come over to the Nisqually Administration ."

As they were talking Hiram's cell rang. He looked at his cell phone. It was Tony D. He hit the green accept button. "Hiram," Tony D said, "think we may have an inroad to the WSDA agent. Yes, there's a man in the Natural Resources Building that wears a goddamn fake leg. I'll try and find out the guy's name. Gotta go." As always, Tony abruptly hung up.

Hiram turned to Gage. "Looks like we're finally in for some rays of light. Tony found out that the bionic dude actually does exist. We just got to get his name, location, and home address. And, you're right, the guy at the Nisqually center seems to have a pretty good game plan to tackle Hafer's fears. But we have to remember what the Buddha-boy kept tellin' his monks: 'Let go of expectations, don't try to control the rock and roll, just roll.'" Hiram smiled. "Or, something like that. So let's go with the flow and run with these two brain-boy ideas on the bionic, and the balloons."

CHAPTER 17

It was mid afternoon and bright flashes appeared above Elliot Bay. Two beautiful hot air balloons were drifting over the bay with sparkling white lights. The lights outlined different messages. One hot air balloon had the words: Chief Seattle was a hero. The second balloon had another bulletin: Chief Leschi was a superstar. The balloons floated over the bustling Pike Place Market, down the Seattle waterfront to the historic Pioneer Square, and finally came back up the waterfront to Steinbrueck Park overlooking the bay. They hovered above the park.

There were six American Indians in each balloon beating their drums in rhythm. The Indians shouted out words of peace and compassion over their loudspeakers.

From the Leschi air balloon came cheers of approval: "When Chief Seattle was fourteen years old he united with a powerful spiritual guide called the Thunderbird. This spirit guided him through his life, teaching him and protecting him as he fought hard battles for his people, and won many encounters."

From the Chief Seattle balloon came love and delight: "On Chief Leschi's birth a shining star appeared over his tribe's territory. It brought a spiritual future to Leschi, guaranteeing him to become his people's warrior chief, savior, and saint."

Many people at the park, and on the waterfront, were looking up into the sky as the words of approval and applause blasted out. Cars were stopping on Alaskan Way, and even stopping on the Viaduct.

From the Leschi balloon came more news: "Chief Seattle's conversion to Christianity marked his emergence as a leader who sought friendship and cooperation with the American settlers."

The Chief Seattle balloon called out: "When settlers began to arrive in the Puget Sound, Leschi was as adept at dealing with them as he had been with the famous Hudson Bay Company. He gained the settlers' confidence as one 'fantastic Indian.'"

The Chief Leschi balloon hit its drums: "We honor Chief Seattle."

The Chief Seattle balloon banged their drums loudly: "We honor Chief Leschi."

KOMO news had rushed to the park and aired the event. Cars drove to the park. Groups of people jammed into the park. The balloons kept buzzing away with friendly facts and felicitations on both sides of the ball game. And of course, tribal music was pouring out everywhere all over the park.

Brice Hafer's phones started ringing wildly. Several people were calling him. He quickly fired up the TV. What the hell was going on? The Chief Seattle crowd is finally giving applause to his Leschi? They're finally crossing the gate of fear and phobia? And the Leschi gang? They're throwing out praise to Chief Seattle, the guy that signed a treaty with the white folks that forfeited his enormous Suquamish land, and jeopardized the freedom of other Indian tribes? This is shit!

Brice called The Inn and was transferred to Gage McClure. "McClure, are you some cheese head? Did you set up those gasbags to get back at me? People are going crazy over the dialogues. The two groups are saluting each other with praise. There are hordes of people in the park looking up at the balloons. I'm stunned."

"No, I didn't set it up. But, I think your Leschi hero can gain even more leverage with a little help. Meet me in front of the hotel, and we'll jam over to the Nisqually Indian Administration and meet with Bert Collin."

"To hell with you. All you do McClure is keep trying to find ways to manipulate and maneuver me."

"Brice, you're the pro at manipulation. You're the one who's tried to blast this hotel apart. You're the one who's demanded to detonate the waterfront—all because of your blue sky desires. Why not get over here, and we'll go see Bert for the best ways to get your goals won."

"Violence McClure. Violence causes more awareness than peace, and more focus than pure harmony. I need to prove the government was wrong; I need to prove it now. I don't want to procrastinate with wishes and words so that the public and the government might one day provide forgiveness, and give Chief Leschi a rebirth. I need violence."

"Brice, no matter how brutal you become, you won't reach unity in Seattle with bloodshed. To get to your goal you need to press on peace with facts and figures, along with some guidance on how to maneuver smoothly. Open your eyes instead of closing your fists."

"Great McClure, you're an educated man with a backlash of bright words. You're filled with these words, but you're lackin' horse sense."

"Damn it, we've argued a million times. Right now, right this minute, can we simply see we're after the same thing: to U-turn one piece of Seattle history. You're Nisqually. I know the head man of the Nisqually Administration. He'll help you. I'll get you over there."

"I've told you I know of him. He may have ability, but the guy's no highbrow. Several of his projects haven't even been accepted by the state."

"Dealing with any government can be challenging at times. But he's got inspiration and insight."

"There you go again, talkin' like a fancy person. I'm not going over to him. And I am going to tear your hotel apart, along with other treasure troves in Seattle for all the wrong that's been done to Chief Leschi, and the stupid praise aimed at Chief Seattle." Brice hung up.

Hiram walked into Gage's office. Gage was looking like a scraped apple. "Just got off the line with Brice," Gage said. "I think the damn voices in his head are going wild. He won't even try to get some guidance from the Nisqually Administration. And he'll start retaliating with more vengeance for all the closed eyes and sins that have been passed down from this state government."

"OK, settle down. We've dealt with him before, we'll do it again. But first some good news to knock the sadness out of your Einstein. I got off the phone with Tony D. He came up with the bonuses. Dillon's co-conspirator in the WSDA is a chump called Zak Nebard. Tony says for sure, he's got a peg leg, a pretty cool bionic leg. The thing is, it makes him move stronger and faster than before he had his leg amputated. He lives alone in a sharp house in Holiday Hills, close to Ward Lake. He's divorced. Before the divorce they lived in a pretty low-level neighborhood. Things are totally different now that he's accepting kickbacks from Dillon. I think it's time to give ol' Dillon a talk about loose money, Nebard, and corporate gambling. We'll go over by plane tomorrow. I think Matt's goin' to get his good life back. Anna will too."

CHAPTER 18

After they got off the plane and taxied to downtown Spokane, they walked into the Bank of America Financial Center building. They went up to the 18th floor and entered Dillon Russell's reception area. "We'd like to see Dillon," Hiram said.

The receptionist blinked her eyes. "I surely don't think Mr. Russell will see you, not with all the trouble you've caused in the past. In fact if you don't leave now, I'll call security."

"Very similar to what you said last time, young lady." Hiram handed her the card with the WSDA agent's name on it. "I am sure Mr. Russell will want to see this. We'll wait quietly."

The lady took the card and went into Dillon's private office. Moments later Dillon walked out with her. "As always Hiram, you do come up with surprises. Why don't the two of you come into my office. But first Hiram—I'd like you to put your gun down on the receptionist's desk. Or, I'll call the backup boys."

Hiram laid his gun on the desk, and the three of them walked into Dillon's office.

Dillon held the note card in his hand. Damn, where did they get Nebard's name? Easy, take it easy. These guys aren't the smartest. But this Hiram animal is genuinely tenacious. "Well, you men seem to get high on interfering with my top-of-the-line tasks."

"You, Mr. Russell, seem to be possessed with a fear of failure."

Dillon shook his head. Was he supposed to believe this cocky kid? "Do you grasp the essentials of business Hiram? Capitalism is an economic system based upon private ownership and the operation for profit. In any capitalist market, decision making and investments are determined by every owner of wealth, whereas prices and services are determined simply by the competition. My decision to increase productivity in the Cle Elum area comes from capitalism. It's practical and profitable. I ask for assistance from the WSDA, and that is practical and productive."

"Asking for advice is great. Advocating corruption, like bribing an agent in the WSDA, sure ain't practical," Hiram said.

"Bribing?" Dillon shouted.

Hiram pointed to the name on the note card.

"Mr. Nebard is a friend who works in the administration. He's not a venal state employee. Sure, he looks up numbers and names to help me know more about the farm lands around Cle Elum and Spokane. And sure, I use the information. But he doesn't do anything illegal. I've already got your Anna, and I'll leave her alone as long as you stop your stunts. When Matt's farm has been bought, I'll move on, and you get Anna back. Stop your efforts and let capitalism work its way. I think it's time to leave."

"That's good Dillon. If we were normal blockheads, if we just accepted your thesis, we'd stand up and go. Problem is Mr. Russell, you're an arrogant shit-head that only sees greenbacks. You lie to the hilt. My friend, Tony D, knows about this Nebard guy. If I call Tony, Nebard will be captured. And, your dollar bill empire with go down the drain once he testifies on the ways you've bribed him to make situations hard for Matt, or for any farmer who won't give up their land to your offers. So back off right now and—"

"You're totally wrong. But if you persist with your narrow minds, and if you do anything that will club me, I'll have your Anna tortured worse than Simmons was." Good God, these men, especially fuckin' Hiram, could destroy his whole enterprise; ruin everything he had built. He'd be crushed. He wouldn't let them defeat him. He wouldn't let them scarp the walls off his hidden activities. "We can go back and forth a zillion times. Only thing is, I don't have the time. Now get out of here, don't do a damn thing to try and become heroes for Matt and you'll get Anna back once everything's on the right track."

"It will be awful if we lose Anna. But drop down a level: you'll be wiped out if Nebard testifies. Plus, you'll end up with fifteen years in prison. So stop your threats, let go of your voracity, and issue a notarized statement to the district court that you will not violate any of Matt's property. Also, make sure Matt's wife will be returned."

Dillon paused, battered some ideas in his head, then pushed his chair away from the desk. "Well, it looks like the meeting's over. I'll get the statement out to the district court, and send you a copy. Anna and Matt's wife will be delivered to the hotel when this is all done. Right now, I've got to get back to work."

"When will you send us the statement?"

"To get my lawyer primed and have him file the document will take a couple of days." The reality was, it would take him less than a day to grab Nebard without their knowledge.

"It's better if you put out full energy and deliver us a copy, no later than a day. One day! Plus, have Anna and Matt's wife delivered to us at the same time."

"You do have doubts. OK, one day it'll be." Hell, he would have the damn man grabbed way before tomorrow. He would have him swiped by tonight. "Now, may we say goodbye?"

As Gage and Hiram walked to the elevator Gage asked, "Will he do what we asked?"

"You never know with guys like Dillon, but I think we have him cornered, so he should follow through. If he doesn't deliver, we react with wild intentions and lawyers."

CHAPTER 19

A car turned off of Yelm Highway and moved onto Village Drive SE with the car lights off. The area was close to Ward Lake in the Holiday Hills community of Olympia Washington, and it was filled with trees and views of the lake. Dillon Russell and two of his security men were in the car. It was in the evening and they were going to give Zak Nebard an unusual invitation. But first they were going to check if there were any suspicious surveillance cars around.

There were none.

The two security guards stayed in Dillon's car. Dillon rang the doorbell and in a minute Zak opened the front door. "Dillon? What the—what are you doing here? You could have called."

"Got some important news. Mind if I come in?"

Zak showed him into the living room.

"As you know there are some men pressing hard to stop my activities with the Matt Hastings' farm. One of the ways is to find you and force you to tell them what information you've given me, and what money I've given you. If they find out, we're in thick mud, buddy. So I think it's wise if you leave this house now, at least for a month. And tomorrow call in sick at the office."

Zak stared at Dillon. He needed Dillon to leave. His life had become full of pellets and odd pressures. Ever since he lost his leg and had an artificial one put on, many people kept looking at him with a slight shade of dislike. He always kept his air of confidence, but there were times he wanted to run away, grab a knife, and ram the damn thing into his eye so he wouldn't keep seeing people's dislike at his artificial leg. "Dillon, I have no idea where to go. I certainly don't have the extra money to stay anywhere for a month."

"Not a problem. I'll take you to a cabin I have. Pack up and we'll leave."

"There's no way I can leave now. And besides, I think you're overdoing it. No one, besides the two of us, knows anything of the harm we've caused to Matt and some other farmers. If you or I get pulled to court, no one can prove anything."

"That's absurd. Get your bags packed. I need to be sure Matt's farm will be included in my system."

"I know you. Hell, I've colluded and conspired with you. You're intense. I went along with you because of your bankrolls. Can't say I'd ever be friends with you, but I won't let anyone know what we've done. Now, if you'd leave."

Dillon spat on the rug and walked out the door. Minutes later he burst back to the house with his bodyguards. Zak was thrown to the wall and cuffed.

CHAPTER 20

Gage was in his suite at The Inn finishing some paperwork. The stars were bright. The water was bewitching. This hotel was his haven, his place of peace. As he opened a desk drawn, there were some strange crackling sounds.

Suddenly from over the bay a loud voice started yelling. Gage jumped up and opened the window. He looked out and spotted a seaplane over the marina. "GAGE McCLURE. YOUR HOTEL IS GOING TO BE SMASED IF YOU DON'T LISTEN TO ME." The seaplane curved to the left and flew away.

The front desk was once again blasted with phone calls from the guests.

Gage's phone rang. He quickly picked up. "Mr. McClure, there is a gentlemen down here in the lobby. A Brice Hafer. He needs to talk with you. Can you come down?"

Hell, it's Brice all over again. This character kept showing up only to do one thing: to promote a dead idol. He knows spit about the green light of cooperation. "I'll come down." Gage hung up the phone and took in a long deep breath.

As Gage came out of the elevator, Brice Hafer was by the front desk. Gage walked over to him. "I think it best we go over to the large chairs by the windows."

"I ain't goin' to sit down, but I'll walk over there and we can talk."

They started walking to the corner area. Gage tightened his face. Why did so many odd people come into his life? Was he being driven by the flow of karma, as Hiram kept saying. Driven by fears and fudge pots from his past? Damn it!

"Mr. McClure, I'm going to blow your place to hell if you don't abide with my wishes. I need this castle of yours to promote the man that matters. Your hotel is a large landmark in Seattle. I need places like yours to kill the admiration for Chief Seattle, and get the green light going for Chief Leschi. We—all of us—need to learn about the guts and glamour of Leshci. Seattle needs to be educated. Your place will be bombed to ashes if you don't construct a statue of Chief Leschi. Are you willing to do this?"

"Brice, you keep saying the same thing, in different ways, each time we meet. And each time you—"

"Gage, shut the fuck up and listen. I have a demolition bomb that's designed to crack apart your hotel. You don't obey me and we drop that bomb. Your place will become dust. Anything—"

Brice was pulled down to the ground, and then Hiram stomped on him. "You were talking so loud, you didn't even hear me come up behind you. Did you? Listen up dude, it ain't polite to threaten people, and it sure ain't too savvy to show people your mask of strength. I think it's best to be kind to yourself above anything else, and then have some heart to the folks outside yourself. Hell, if you're after gold or a goal Brice, it's wise to collaborate versus clash with the crowd you wanna deal with. Am I making any sense?"

"What? Are you here to sound off like some college professor who can't get a real job in the real world. Get the hell off me."

"Will do, if you sit down on one of these chairs, instead of standing up like an e-tard."

"Like a what?"

"Skip it. Sit down on one of the club chairs. You too, Gage. Let's have a little talk." Hiram got off Brice and sat down on another club chair. "OK, what's up Brice?"

"Hiram, you're ridiculous. I ain't here to talk. I've done that before and you guys don't listen worth shit. You can beat me up, toss me out a window, but I need you men to get a crew over here tomorrow. Tomorrow. And start building a statue. A ten feet tall figure."

"Ten feet tall?"

"All right. All right. Skip the ten feet. Just start building."

"And if we don't, you're going to crash this hotel with a bomb? Cute Brice, but sick."

"Maybe sick to you, but it puts you to the limit, ass hole. You need to get some hired shovels workin' like mad men tomorrow and construct an icon."

"Brice, you keep slamming out your desires. This is Seattle. Biggest city in the state. We've got police, armed aircraft, armed boats, and plane detectors. And we can notify the city right now. If there's any kind of explosion here, you'll be found. Jail term will be up to fifteen years. Get it!"

"Hiram, you can go round and round, but there ain't no way they'll prove it will be me, no matter how much you do your fancy talkin'. You're nothin' but a pipe-man, and I have all—"

"The only way you can't get caught is if I slam the hell out of you right now. You'll be dead meat, and we just toss ya in the bay."

"For God's sake! All I want is to have a man, who was wrongly hung by this State Government, become free. It's over a hundred years and this government hasn't done anything. They're like you: they talk a lot but do nothing on the real issue."

Brice looked at Gage, then back toward Hiram. "Both of you guys are just dipshits. Hiram, if you want to scare me, go for it! If you want to kill me, go for it! If you're made up of more than fast talk and shit-ass threats, then—pull out your pistol and shoot the bullets into my face. But I don't think you have the true intention to do that, do you?" Brice turned, went past the front desk, and left.

Gage looked at Hiram. Hiram stared back at Gage.

CHAPTER 21

Matt and his two sons arrived in Seattle late in the day. He drove to The Inn at the Pier and were waiting for Gage by a small pond in the lobby. The kids were splashing each other with water. Matt was smiling. His boys were his gift. His wife was a cherished gift, too. And finally she'd be released today, after being kidnapped for a month. He tightened his hand on the chair. He would now be able to return to the wide open space of farm living. He'd be able to create the fire of intimacy with his family again. And he'd be able to go back to the joy of nature and nurturing animals. Once more, the land of sunshine and love would circle his farm.

Gage walked over to the pond and put his hand on Matt's shoulder. "Matt, no one is allowed within ten feet of the pond. Didn't you read the sign right there?" Matt squinted to where Gage was pointing. He looked alarmed. Gage started laughing. "I'm joking. It's a joke. Gotta have some humor in this place or it'll all crash in. Come on big-guy, let's go to my office."

The boys and the men got on the elevator, went into the office, and everyone sat by the giant windows overlooking the bay. The waves were small but wonderful, and the sky was romantic as a dream within a dream.

"You're probably as happy as I am about your wife," Gage said. "As I told you over the phone, Hiram and I went to Dillon's place.

The conversation got tough, but we did make several agreements. Your land and your wife were tops on the agenda. A court approved document that your land won't be solicited any more should arrive today, and your wife—thank God—will also be delivered to our hotel today." Gage gave a glance at his watch. "Why don't we all go for a walk by the marina?"

As they were walking along the floating walkway Hiram came running up to them. "Gage, damn it, Tony called. Zak's been captured. Taken away. It's been done by Dillon. I called Dillon on his cell. He answered, with some fuckin' calmness and tranquility. I asked what the hell happened to Zak. He said the man has gone away for good. So Matt will have to give up his resistance. If he doesn't, dear Cindy will be gone for good; same goes for Anna. He said at the end, to have Matt give him a call so he can receive the money Dillon's always offered him for the farm. And, Anna would be raped hard by his men, for a year, then killed if Gage won't stop all of his actions in all of this. Dillon hung up after that."

Gage shut his eyes. Matt grabbed the railing. He could jump over now. Be done with it all. Matt looked at the boys. They were hugging his legs and crying. "Where's momma? Where is she?" Matt knew he couldn't let go of life. Not while his boys were still young and growing up. Where would he go after he gave the farm to Dillon? The money the man kept offering would only buy a small farmland, hardly enough to live on. But, Cindy! He needed her. He couldn't do what Dillon demanded. But he had to! Matt's body shook as he kept crying next to his boys. And his tears kept falling onto them.

"Hiram, get a moveable chair from the lobby. Bring it here quickly."

Gage pulled Matt closer to the boys, then he sat down on the walkway and held everyone's hands. The tears kept coming. "Matt, we're both trapped. But somehow we're going to get our girls back."

Minutes later Hiram came with the movable chair. Matt sat down and the kids sat on his lap. Hiram and Gage wheeled the group into the hotel and up to a warm corner suite. After Matt and the children had showered, the little boys crashed into bed. While they were sleeping Hiram, Gage, and Matt went over to the suite's wall of windows, sat down, and gazed out to the bay for some peace. "Matt," Hiram said," this is tough, but we're going to make it through. Guaranteed. The man called Tony D might give us some direction to all this. Gage and I gotta get down to the office right now and figure things out. You get some sleep good buddy, or just keep looking out the magic widows to the bay for a while and relax. We'll see you in the morning."

CHAPTER 22

Anna was locked in Dillon's mansion, sitting on a small couch in the room she had been thrown into. How was she going to get out of this mess? She couldn't be tortured by some of Dillon's guys. She couldn't be thrown against the wall, raped, and slapped on her ass with chain belts. Was life a damn mystery, filled with moments, or even days, of fun then slammed into corners of dread and doubts? Was her life molded together by the sleazy upbringing she had as a homeless child? Was she destined for hell, or could she gain the guts to break out of her mushroom mental mind? She threw her shoe into a mirror and began looking around the room. With a lot of effort she pulled apart a short-legged table next to the wall. Anna quickly placed one of the legs of the table on the floor next to the couch, and took off her clothes so her breasts and body looked like a wild version of pop art. She banged loudly and steadily against the door, waiting for one of Dillon's guards to appear.

Soon the door opened. The fuckin' guard looked like he saw a goblin or some smooth skin made of booger sugar. His eyes were airy and wide.

"Please help me," Anna yelled. "I have cold feet and I'm worried sick as to what's going on." She forced some tears. "I got panic-stricken and tore off my clothes, and slapped my face." She dove into the guard's body. "Please take me to the couch and help me calm down. Please!" She hugged the guard tightly. Anna forced her bosoms against his face. Her nipples swished across his mouth.

The guard was definitely confused; his faced was wrinkled, but he roughly carried her to the couch, and—

Anna had picked up the wooden table leg and smashed his head. Twice. The guard fell onto the floor. Knocked out cold.

What was she doing? She had never done this before: stripped naked, plastered her tits across a guy's face, and slammed his head with a club. Anna fell back on the couch. Why did she ever get into this nightmare? Who the hell was she? A damn whore who was trying to get free of the scars and scrapes of a backstreet life?

She was doing all this to help Gage out of his mess, so he'd thank her and continue to help her out of her mess? He gave her the praise she couldn't give herself. Anna twisted and turned as she kept wiping her eyes.

After a few minutes she got up and rifled through the guard's pockets. Took out some keys and a cell phone. Along with his gun. She put on her dress, strapped on some shoes, opened the door, and carefully looked up and down the hallway. Cautiously she went to the next door and knocked softly. "Aaron, Aaron, you there?"

A mumbled voice came back to her. "Anna, is that you?" Anna tried several keys on the key chain. Finally, one worked. She opened the door. Aaron was white as a ghost as he held out both his hands. "How, did you get out from the room? I heard a lot of banging."

"We'll talk later. Right now, we got to find a way out of here. Are there back stairs to this blasted mansion?"

"Follow me."

They went down the hallway. As they started to open the door, guards came running down the hallway. Anna dashed through the door. Aaron came right after her, but was shot in the hip and fell down. Anna started to turn around, but more shots were fired. She ran down two flights of stairs and out a door. As she kept running she passed a laundry room. She stopped, turned her head, then ran back into the room. She jammed open the door to the dryer, knocked away a level bar and squeezed herself in, shutting the door loosely.

Was she in a movie that would never be released? A movie so unbelievable it would be a cheap fiction flick. No one would want to watch it. Hell, she had to get out of here. She couldn't be tortured or pumped by perverts. How was she going to find her way? If she was captured she'd be forced to hold onto the one belief that kept running through her: she was worthless. The only reason anyone looked at her was because of her body, it had nothing to do with respect, kindness, or confidence. Those were completely absent in her. Was this always going to be true? Her voice kept telling her: you're cheap shit. Anna closed her eyes while tears ran over her face. Go on, crawl out of the dryer, walk into the hallway, and give yourself up. You're a waste.

SHUT UP, her other voice yelled back. Anna shook her head. Fuuuck! She tried listening for any noise outside the door. Nothing. She had to get out of here. She listened again. No noise from any of the guards. She was on the first floor. All she had to do was break out of this knothole dryer, go down one floor, and get out some back door.

She dragged herself out of the dryer, and listened. Oh damn, now there were noises. There were mumbling men in the hallway. She wiggled back into the dryer and pulled out the cell phone she took from the guard, pressed some numbers, and waited a couple seconds. "Gage, my God, what a nightmare. I'm stuffed in a damn dryer in Dillon's mansion. Hopefully I'll be safe for a while. No—Aaron's been captured. Look, I need you and Hiram to find the address of this place from Simmons, and get over here quickly. The place ain't guarded. But be quiet and sneaky. Find a way to go through the locked gate, ignite a larger-than-hell fire with some explosives by the side of this massive wooden mansion, and then call the fire department. Have them get over here. When they're here there'll be wild chaos, then I'll come out the backstairs. Be there waiting for me." Anna closed the cell phone and covered her face with her hands.

Gage turned to Hiram and explained the whole idea.

"Anna's an ace," Hiram said. "OK, I'll get the gas cans filled and ready. We'll also bring along the backpack sprayers and plenty of crude oil. Give me half an hour and I'll meet you at the front door." Hiram left.

Gage closed his eyes. What normal guy has his life colored with so much hot water and bad news? He shook his head and remembered Hiram's motto: 'Ain't nothing stays certain Gage, so learn ta flow.' Gage half smiled, as he finished his paper work on the desk.

Hiram met Gage out front in a Ford Ranger. Off they went to Dillon's mansion. It would be about a four hour drive.

When they arrived at Dillon's mansion Hiram turned off the headlights, and stopped about twenty feet before the gate. He got out, attached two mufflers to the engine, walked over to the gate, and put a knife into the bottom half of the keyhole. He applied pressure first in one direction then in the other. The lock gave a bit; he applied a little more pressure, then he opened the gate and looked around. It was safe so far. He got back in the truck. They went to the south side of the house where there were only windows three floors up. They took out the large gas cans, along with the backpack sprayers. After filling the backpack sprayers, they went to different ends of the south side and started spraying the wood with gas. Soaking it. Then the big event: they ignited all the wood, and it exploded with flames of fire all over the south side. Both of them rushed back to the truck, and drove to a cluster of trees. Hiram called the local fire department, telling them there was an emergency at the mansion, come quickly. He then called Anna on the stolen cell phone and told her to listen for the sirens. "Anna when you hear the sirens, go down the backstairs, but be careful there's going to be panic and confusion."

Yelling came from the front of the house. Windows were being smashed open. Men were running around the front of the mansion to the fire on the side of the home. The fire had reached the third floor. The south side of the house was burning and crackling like hell. Sirens started screeching loudly as the fire engines came through the gate. Guards pointed to the side of the building. The trucks blasted to the south side. As the crews from the two fire trucks were opening the pump panels and raising the aerial ladders, Anna dashed out from the back of the mansion. Gage was waiting for her, and took her to another round of trees. He held her strongly as he called Hiram on his cell.

Hiram slowly drove the Ford Ranger to Gage and Anna. They jumped in. As he drove toward the front gate, gun shots opened up. Hiram ducked down, pulling Anna down, as he continued to zigzag on toward the gate. They made it through. Hiram kept driving past the first turn, then stopped, jumped out and opened Gage's door. "Holy crackers, it sure got a little touchy there at the end."

Hiram climbed up a tree. "Gage, take a look at that fire. It's gone wild." Hiram looked down to Anna. "Anna, you escaped! You're free! And Dillon's house is red-hot. I love you babe."

Gage started hugging her.

Hiram climbed down the tree, came over and hugged both of them. "Anna," Hiram said, "all I can do is thank the Gods you're a boomtown babe with brass. I thank every star in the heavens that you came to our hotel so I could get to know ya." He kissed her hard. She started crying. "Come on, let's get back to The Inn."

CHAPTER 23

Simmons came out the front door of The Inn as the Ford Ranger came onto the driveway. When the bulky pickup truck stopped, she opened the door, bent down, and grabbed Anna. "Precious, I need you in my life so much. I was frightened you were roped and hammered like I was in his goddamn mansion."

"They did nothing to me. I was put in a room, but no one came in. I remained safe. Yet I was scared out of my mind that at any hour they would come in and do some gang banging."

Simmons kissed her again and again.

They all walked into the hotel and went over to the front desk. Hiram talked with the front desk manager for a moment, then gave Simmons a room key. "Simmons take Anna up to this master suite, get her a glass of beer, and get her hot tub ready. Then tuck her into bed after she dries off. You may want a hot bath too before you jump into the second bedroom." Hiram turned to Anna and kissed her with warmth and wonder. "Have a great sleep, Miss Marvelous."

Simmons went with Anna to the master suite.

Hiram turned to Gage. "Come with me, we need to call Matt. While we were waiting for Anna to come out of Dillon's damn mansion, I was thinking about Matt's problem with Dillon. I think there's another way to tackle that cowboy." He looked at his watch. "It's late but not that bad. Let's give Matt a call."

They were in Gage's room as Hiram made a call to Matt. "Howdy Matt, sure hope I didn't wake ya up. I was thinking there might be something else we can do to help get Cindy back home, and keep Dillon off your back. Matt, do you know if there's another property Dillon is pursuing? Is there anyone close to you on the farm lands that are also struggling with Dillon?"

"Actually Hiram, there are several. Dillon is trying hard to widen his advantage. One I know the most about is Abbot Tindol. We've talked about our beloved families, our farms, and the agricultural economy. He's been in conflict with Dillon for almost five months. His farm is not as big as mine, so the lower money Dillon is offering is not that enticing. Abbot is roughly twenty miles from my farm. And his farm is under economic pressure, like mine is. Price crashes for corn, wheat, dairy, beef and other darn products have made a sharp plunge in farm income. Dillon knows this, that's why he's tempting us with immediate cash. Dillon wants a giant farm corporation, and is determined to wipe us out to gain that corporation. Abbot wants to stay in farming, but he's not sure how he can."

"Matt, this is some damn good info. Let me get back to you." Hiram turned off his phone. "Gage, I think we just might have an opening. I'm gonna give Tony a call in the morning."

The next morning a couple of workmen were constructing a shiny wooden floor on the north end of the pier. Other workmen were installing some cable railings on the same section of the pier. Gage was determined to create an outdoor nightclub. He wanted people in Seattle to have a place where they could have fun and forget about thoughts and issues for a while. The view was eye-catching and daring.

As Gage was talking to one of his employees, Hiram came out of a side door of The Inn. "Gage, got some Tony news. Come on over to the railing."

They walked to the water railing. "Tony has contacted this Abbot Tindol character. Abbot and Tony talked about Matt's danger with

Dillon, and Tindol's danger with Dillon. They came up with a plan. Abbot is going to call Dillon's office and tell them he wants no more to do with Dillon. He's had enough tension. He's going to put his farm up for sale—for anyone but Dillon—and use that money to buy another farm far away from Dillon. Most likely Dillon, or some of his men, will come over to Abbot's farm and apply pressure to stop Abbot's actions. No matter who shows up, we'll have some of Tony's guys inside Abbot's farm ready to corral Dillon or his men."

CHAPTER 24

Abbot's office had called Dillon. Dillon called Abbot. "Abbot, my office notified me. You seemed pretty distressed and upset over the phone. In reality, your message would only spark more of our friction. I could crush anyone who would try and buy your farm. And then, I'd press down even harder on your land. So, let's try another way. We could make a swap and lower the tension. You give me your land, and I'll give you one of my farm lands on N. Gerlach, in Spokane. It's sixty-five acres, with some view of the mountains. I'm not widening my interests in that area. In fact it's the only land I have in that sector. Your farm and Matt's farm, and all the land around both of yours, is what holds interest for me. You can keep on farming with your love and passion on the Gerlach land. And I'll keep on doing what I love to do with fury and fever. This way we both win. Think about it. I'll get back to you." The call ended.

Abbot bit his teeth and walked out to the wooden porch. The view from the porch was tremendous. Farming was his joy. Would he ever leave this ranch? No. Yes. No. Well, maybe. It might be the best way to break out of Dillon's threats and pressures. Was Dillon being truthful? What the hell would Matt say? Matt was under blocks of burden, just like he was. Matt was losing his live stock because there wasn't enough coins in his bag of bucks. And he had no more backup money. He was getting low on fertilizers and pesticides. His wheat and barley were sinking. And he was giving half his time to defending Dillon's threats of corporate farming. His cows and sheep were existing but needed much more attention.

Farming used to be such a joy for both of them. Abbot knew it. Should he take Dillon's offer and believe the asshole wouldn't walk out on the guarantee? But if he did take the offer, wouldn't that increase the pressures and problems on Matt? More corporate land would be surrounding Matt.

Abbot rubbed his hands and hit the side of the chair.

If he refused Dillon's offer, wouldn't Dillon, or some of his men, come over and try to force him to accept the offer? Then wouldn't this Hiram guy be able to capture them and force Dillon to stop all his nonsense? Maybe Dillon would even be sent to jail? And then wouldn't he and Matt both be able to go back to the dream of farming with far-reaching fields and wild sunsets?

Abbot called Dillon back. "Mr. Russell, I can't take your offer. I'm selling my farm. The realtor will push hard." Abbot hung up.

Matt's cell phone started ringing. It was his wife. "Matt sweetheart, I needed to, I had to call you." Cindy started crying over the phone. "Dillon said if I didn't call you I'd be murdered. Help me. I beg you, please let Dillon have our land. When you do that I can be released from this place of hanging knives and fat men that keep slapping my ass. We need to get our family united again. Our children are precious. You are. This place is a nightmare. Matt, yesterday he—"

Dillon grabbed the phone from her. "Well, Mr. Hastings, seems you've been looking at the mirror backwards. All the help that McClure and his fucked up muscle man have given you has only ended in more people getting hit with turmoil. Your wife will be swimming in blood baths if you don't do one thing: Turn your land over to me, immediately. No more wasting time. No more calling Gage or Hiram or any of the farmers in your area. Let me know soon, or you'll be toast." Dillon hung up.

Matt phoned Gage and told him the goddamn horror story.

"Matt, this is hell," Gage said. "And yes, we're going to find a way out! I'm going to call Hiram and give him the details. But right now, I want you and the boys to get over here now. I want you resting in comfort. You'll be in a warm water suite."

Gage walked over to Hiram's office. Hiram was sitting on a thick windowsill looking out toward the bay as he was doing some paper work. Gage told him about Matt's terror.

"Gage, what we need to do is to counter attack Dillon's demands." Hiram looked away from the window. "We need to apply extra pressure on Dillon. That's why I had Tony D call Abbot. We need to have both farm lands handed over to you. Abbot's and Matt's. Dillon will be stuck."

"That's good. It has some taste, but we've got the other problem: Cindy is being held captive. If we do the damn transferring of the farms, won't she be beaten up, or even killed, as some kind of payback for our action?"

"Not if we apply more pressure than he can handle. Given all he's done with Simmons and Anna, and so far with Cindy, we'll get hold of our lawyer. We let Mike know what the hell Dillon's done, and have him come up with a felony charge of a couple years in prison. We tell Dillon that if he doesn't let Cindy go, our lawyer is going to tackle him with jail time."

"Will . . . will he buy that?"

"Probably not till he sees the damn legal document in black and white. We'll get Mike working on it. Right now, we've got some homework to do to get those two lands transferred over to you."

Gage shook his head. "I'm worried like hell about Matt. He needs security. He needs his family. These are good ideas you have. But no one can predict the future to anything. All of this can turn crazy, given Dillon's mind. Matt could end up in a dark disaster."

"Gage, I've told ya this a million times: You're right. You can't control the world, or any fuck'n situation in it. But ya can control your reactions to what's happenin'. What's that old song: 'Cowgirls

Don't Cry.' Same goes for you, hold tight." Hiram hit Gage on the shoulder. "Come on cowboy, let's get a little shut-eye. Tomorrow we'll start the struggle to save Matt."

CHAPTER 25

It was 9 at night, a big tug boat with speakers was moving to the north end of Gage's hotel. "Everyone. Get out of your rooms and run out of the hotel."

Blasts of bloodcurdling screams came out of the boat's speakers.

"Get out of the hotel. It's going to be blown apart. Hands, feet, heads will fly over the dock from the explosions about to happen."

The phones rang like mad at the front desk. The night manager had already called Gage and Hiram. Some of the guests were coming out of the elevator, others were running down the stairs and out the front doors. More phones were ringing. Hiram came down the backstairs to the front desk.

Gage came down the other backstairs. Was Dillon doing this? No way. Had to be Brice? Gage cringed. No one lived a life like he did. Gage ran over to Hiram. "Do you have a clue to any of this?" Gage wiped his damn face.

"Don't have a clue Gage. But no matter what, get Dale over here quickly, plus call Harry at the cop station. Have him jet over here with some men. And we need Randy to get here with his construction crew." They both went into the front desk office.

Gage started making his calls. This was out of a damn soap opera. A hotel filled with—

"Gage," the front desk guy yelled into the speaker. "Gage, take line three. Someone's demanding to talk to you."

Gage picked up the phone. "McClure! You're about to be ruined! Got it! But I'll hold off on my actions if, and only if, you do one thing: When the local TV stations send their news crew over to film what-the-hell is going on, I want you to firmly state that all this chaos has to do with a misconduct the city of Seattle and Washington State has not dealt with for decades. It's all about Chief Leschi and his execution. You tell the cameras that Leschi needs to be exonerated and held in honor by different landmarks in Seattle. All destruction of Seattle's buildings and piers will stop—or continue—if his exoneration is not made. Are you getting this McClure? I'll stop my actions for right now, but I'll watch the TV to see that you give out this information." Brice hung up.

Gage turned to Hiram. "That was Brice. He gave us his usual order: Get Chief Leschi to be exonerated or we're toast. When the TV crew show up I'm supposed to deliver the request for all of Seattle to honor Chief Leschi."

"Sure, do it, but not in any panic way. Talk to the interviewer in a cool, practical way. But before they come, get on the phone and give a call to Bert Collin at the Nisqually Indian Administration. You said they're working on reclaiming Leschi's reputation. Get some probabilities from Bert, and use them in the interviews. OK, we need to calm down the guests, and if they want, get them over to the Hilton. Then I'm going to give Tony a call and see if he has any ideas and connections to setup even better protection for The Inn in case Brice really does try a burst and burn. When we get all this done, and if tomorrow becomes normal again, I'll give ol' Dillon a call about the transfer of ownership of both farm lands over to you."

The TV news crew was all set up in the hotel lobby to interview Gage McClure. The woman reporter came over to Gage. "Mr. McClure, things seem to be settling down. But the situation has been terrible. And, this is also the second time that disaster has hit your hotel. You used to be on the top of the list of exceptional hotels in Seattle. You are unfortunately now dropping down on the list. Why can't you stop such disorder? Why do you put up with this mayhem? Why do you let it continue?"

"Ma'am," Gage said, "your questions seem a bit harsh. We certainly are not putting up with this turmoil. We're finding the root cause to this trouble and tackling it. We've—"

"Tackling it? Mr. McClure, many guests have dashed out of your hotel already. And the first episode, a couple weeks ago, was filled with piercing sounds that also woke up the guests. I wouldn't say you are tackling the problem."

She certainly wasn't the only one lost in this chaos. But he needed to gain some kind of control in this wreck of worries. "Ma'am, it seems there's a political undercurrent that is moving beneath all this havoc. I've been told we may be an unusual target for waking up some kind of trouble that happened long ago in Seattle."

The woman reporter squinted her eyes. "You seem to be off the track, Mr. McClure. Whatever your theory is, all your guests may kiss your cheek because of your smart talk, but they still will demand payback from the awful night they had here."

"'Ma'am, would you slow down just a little? Ever hear of the name, Chief Leschi? He was a revered icon of the Nisqually Indians of Washington. He was convicted in the killing of an army officer in an 1855 war. There are many people today insisting that Chief Leschi was wrongly put to death for supposedly killing that man. And, they want others to realize this. They want a new historical trial made possible."

"What in heaven's name does this have anything to do with the utter chaos that is happening in your hotel?"

He was damn thankful he had called Bert Collin before the interview. "I have spoken to the head of the Nisqually Indian Administration, Bert Collin. He says that it seems there are descendants of Leschi that think since my hotel is talked about often in the media, and is one of the key landmarks on the Seattle waterfront, this hotel could be a stimulus to raise attention to Chief Leschi— if—this hotel could be focused on, and would start advocating Chief Leschi's name and reputation."

"Mr. McClure, that's insane. Do you really think "they" want to use your hotel as a means to draw attention to Chief Leschi, even though you aren't related to him in any way? And, they certainly are using this hotel in a bombastic way."

"Well, this is a mystery of misuse. That's for certain. We'll buckle down hard and find out who did this mess. That's my problem, and it has to be taken care of immediately. But, move forward a little, you should talk to Mr. Collin about Leschi. You'll find out he is now processing a mountain of information surrounding a momentum to gain Chief Leschi's fame. He is going to start rapid inroads to clear Chief Leschi's name and reputation. And, he will need great support from you, and all the media, to recorrect the decision of hanging Leschi in 1885. In fact tomorrow he's going to contact all the chief executives of all television stations and newspapers here in Seattle."

She seemed startled, because this was all new to her. Oh yeah, young ladies that look sexy aren't always sagacious.

Brice Hafer was looking at the TV. He was filled with pride. After the interview was over he shot a call to Gage. "You did well. You gave out some good facts on Leschi, and good efforts to try and fix Leschi's name and fame. Let's see what happens. In the meantime, it might be time to turn over your hotel to me. We can have the transfer done today. I'll be—"

"Brice, slow down. You heard what I said to the TV woman: Bert Collin is working on getting the news out on Chief Leschi. And he's working hard on having the government take steps to exonerate the man. Things are starting to gel, so don't blast out that you'll take over The Inn."

"McClure, I'm putting my strategies in stages. I need control of your hotel to promote Chief Leschi—through different actions I'll do to your hotel, and different promotions I'll be using with your hotel. Then I need to see if the people in Seattle are finally uniting with who Leschi really was: a warrior of wisdom. Not like Chief Seattle, who was purely a sly seeker of sanctions. But, if Bert doesn't come through, I need to start destroying the Seattle waterfront."

"Brice, you're not taking this hotel, no matter how—"

"McClure, did you read the papers last week, and will you listen to the news tonight: Your hotel is being slammed. You're losing guests and reputation. You won't be able to stand another catastrophe. Now get on board and hand over your ownership. Now!"

What the hell was happening? Did Gage have the courage to bust through this shit? He told himself he did, but did he? All right, calm down. Don't think of the negative, think of new roads to move on. Damn it, new ways to open up old roads.

"Brice, there's always more than one way to hit a target. The Inn is an attraction, yes, but it doesn't flash in the minds of all Seattleites. We could popularize Leschi in ALL the arenas and markets Bert and his people could create. His organization could then market Leschi's name in those areas. Chief Leschi's reputation could then be circling all through the Seattle area, and throughout the whole state of Washington. Come on, give it a try."

"If it were possible, it would have already been done. You're an idealist, not footed in reality. I also think your precious dream hotel is going to get ruined, even if I don't take it over. Which I will. Look for some more explosions, and more of your guests rushing away from your hotel." Brice hung up.

Gage hit the desk. What would he do, what could he do to stop Brice? How could he maneuver around this maniac? He had to save The Inn. He had to save his guests. His whole life was tied to this home plate of passion. He pounded his forehead.

CHAPTER 26

The next day Hiram made 'the' call to Dillon Russell. He kept waiting like a bent tree until Dillon answered. "Mr. Russell, Hiram Smith here. I'm calling to update you on what's going on. You definitely seem driven to create a corporation of farmlands in Kittitas County. It appears you need Matt's and Abbot's land to tie your other farmlands together, but they aren't handing over their properties to you. You've kidnapped Matt's wife to force him to give you his land. What you'll try and do next to Abbot, I have no—"

"So, once again Mr. Smith, Matt has contacted you, even though I've told him not to. It looks as if the more he fights my wishes, the more trouble he gets himself into. I suggest you get off the phone, and not try and help Matt any further. The more you help him, the more he's going to be hurt. Goodbye Mr. Smith."

"Dillon," Hiram yelled out, "Matt's farm and Abbot's farm have already been sold!"

"What!"

"Yup, Gage has bought both of them. The deeds will be transferred to him today. It might be, that you're traveling the wrong road. What's that ol' saying: 'the more you're drinkin', the more you can't stop drinkin'.' Same goes for greed. Anyway, Gage will have the farms and he won't hand them over to you, no matter how much you're offering."

"Glad you're confident Hiram. Glad things are going your way. Only one thing to keep in mind: cute Cindy is tied up and can be easily be burned to death in one of the stables, or just thrown down the cliff, if you don't stop your wild actions. Hand the farms over to me, and I'll pay you what I first offered Matt and Abbot. And I'll release Cindy. But, muscle man, if you don't do this, then goodbye Cindy."

"Figured you might say something like this, Dillon. You need to know the obvious: we can quickly charge you with—"

"Hiram, get smart. First, before anything, cops will have to find me. That will be impossible. You've tried and failed. And, if you do try again, I won't wait, I'll have Cindy murdered. So be wise. Get the land titles signed and documented. Have them delivered to my mansion. I'm not there of course, but they'll be given to me. Got it."

"Dillon, there's one more thing to chew on. All your activity and your corporation will be under constant legal watch. Plus, there will be a legal filing to have the State take over your lands. Sure, you will not be captured, as you say, but you will be without income. Your present bank accounts—all of them—will be confiscated. Got it! You won't be dead, but you'll be ruined."

"Interesting Hiram. Another threat? How about something even a little more interesting: part of your hotel has been bombed recently. By whom? I don't know. Most of Seattle doesn't know. That woman reporter sure didn't know. But I'll find out and deal with the person to create a different bombing that'll demolish your place permanently. Your hotel will be dust if you don't comply with my request."

Hiram kicked the table. "Dillon, no matter where you are, I'll find a way to crack your door. Just deliver Cindy to the hotel, or you'll—"

Dillon hung up.

Oh yeah, Hiram was going to have to get ready for a creative canoe ride down some risky rapids.

Hiram walked into Gage's office and told him about the phone call.

"Damn Dillon," Gage said, as he hit the desk. "He's doing it again. Threats upon threats. He's going to find out who Brice is and team up with him to blow this place apart. Great! Now we're threatened by two idiots with egos that fight with the need to be right."

They both looked out to the bay for a little peace. Gage had to get The Inn free from both these eccentric men. He closed his eyes, trying to gain some property of peace. He breathed in and out, deeply, then turned his chair and called Brice. Finally Brice picked up. "Brice, thanks for answering. Obviously you got as mad as a pig-nosed rat on that last idea, thinking all I threw back was soft soap. I've come up with a different angle that might be more down-to-the-ground. How about—"

"Shut the hell up. I want your goddamn place so I can soon use it as a tool, then blow it apart. The city may then actually start believing I can blow the whole waterfront apart. Finally, they actually may start listening to me."

"Sure, there's logic there. But, if you open your eyes wider, there may be a way that helps all of us, and not ruin The Inn. How about if I promote The Inn as a way to gain more respect for Chief Leschi's reputation? Come on over at noon tomorrow, and I'll show you a plan of building statues, not one, but several different ones around the hotel so people can visually incorporate them into all of Elliott Bay, into all of Seattle's waterfront, and into the truth of Seattle's history. We can have signs of his diligence and integrity, his guts and grit, attached to these different carved figures."

"And who the hell is going to build them?"

"I will. I realize now how dedicated that tribal guy was to keeping and flourishing his land."

"All of a sudden you've been struck by the truth? You never listened to me before. Always needing your way, your narrow view of this reality. You make no sense. Why Mc Clure, have you changed your vision?"

"It sure hasn't been because of your hostility. I did research. I've also talked to Bert Collin several times. And even though you shoot from the hip with anger, you're right, the city of Seattle, all of Washington State, really does owe Leschi exoneration."

An awkward hum drowned both ends of the phone.

"Come on over at noon tomorrow," Gage said, "and I'll show you my idea. If you don't like, then leave. You like it, I'll show you more details."

"Once again Gage, you make sense, and you don't make sense. But I'll shoot on over at noon." Brice hung up.

Gage turned to Hiram. "Brice is coming over tomorrow."

Hiram gave him a couple punches on the shoulder. "You're a guy with guts, my friend."

Later that day Hiram met with Anna in his office at The Inn. They were out on the office balcony overlooking the bay. Sailboats were catching the wind, families were out on the docks, and almost everyone was looking up at Mt. Rainier. Hiram waved his arms across the balcony. "This place not only has class, but it's saved my ass when I emerged from prison life. The Inn is my mother and guardian. And if not directly, it's close to the guardian of your life. Anna, I need your hand once more to help ease the trouble surrounding our hotel."

"What do you mean?"

"You know what I mean. You ran into Gage's office when the damn threats came screaming down from the sky last night. And, our guests were rushing down the elevators and out the front doors. It's the jerk called Brice Hafer who caused all this shit. He wants The Inn turned over to him so he can use our place to somehow promote that dead Indian, Chief Leschi. Gage is going to talk with Brice and give him a down-to-earth way to get what he wants for Leschi without killing our place. I need you to help influence Brice into accepting Gage's offer."

141

"You need my help? Am I supposed to go out and throw dough-nuts at the next tug boat captain he uses to crash our piers with bombs and screams? Hiram, from time to time you act like a jerk: Asking me to do something insane, all by myself. Asking me to do a task that can either get me scared or scarred."

Hiram almost smiled. "I'm askin' you to give a listen for a second, and maybe help The Inn, the place that gives us security and a roof over your head filled with love and learning."

Anna stopped looking at Hiram and stared out to the bay. This man was full of heart, yet he had a habit of harm, probably coming from his prison days. But he sure had passion. "Hiram, I've done a couple of your big deeds, and sometimes have gotten caught. Been hit in the face, and sometimes sexually abused. But somehow I deliver, and I keep coming back to The Inn, because of just what you say: It's my home, and the gang that works here is my family. "She threw her hands around him. "All right, how can I help?"

"Gage has offered Brice, at different times, different ways to help bring attention to the wrong that was done to this Chief Leschi character. But every time Brice refused Gage's ideas, and came back with more angered action. This last action of his was outrageous. It's spread all over our local papers. We can't have this happen again, or we could get ruined."

Anna licked her lips.

"Gage has a new plan. It's all centered around our hotel's position and priority here in Seattle. But I need you to delicately influence Brice into accepting this plan."

"Delicately! Hiram, I can do what I've done before: help apply pressure. I can have a bastard fuck me to make him give me a car, a pussy palace, or the info you and Gage need. But I got no skill in the area of delicacy. I ain't no love-dolly gal. I got tits and ass, but no idea of the soft songs and sweet words that make a tough man feel like a butterfly 'bout to cry. You pickin' the wrong maid, babe."

"I don't think so. I ain't been to Harvard or Vanderbilt, but I've been educated on the rough road of life. I know what kicks ass, and blows soft wind. I've been around the block Anna, and I know you have more creativity than any college queen at Columbia. Come on, let's do this, and save our Garden of Eden. I love ya, and I trust you all the way."

Damn it, somehow she knew he'd uncover her. Hiram had what few politicians have: real heart behind his words. "How do I meet this man, and what the hell am I supposed to do to him besides showin' off my hooters?"

"The main thing is to attract him, not just in sexy looks, but also with some sweetness and light."

"With what? What the hell does that mean?"

"It means the exact opposite of what you're doing right now. We'll think of a way for you to create an incident with Brice. And then have you respond to that incident in a way that ain't reactive but almost personal, with a whisper of apology. This'll fascinate him because all he's use to lately are stiff people. And then Anna, somehow, you talk about the power and prominence this hotel has in Seattle."

Anna fumed. This was straight out of a nickel movie made in the Bronx. Ya can't corner a dude with one petty pussy look shining all over your face, send out an apology, and then talk about The Inn like a king cobra house of beds. She shoved her hand toward Hiram's neck—then stopped. And slapped her face instead. Hmm, maybe she could do this. Maybe Hiram was right. Hell, he grew up in the Bronx. Maybe he knew all about five card stud poker.

The next day Anna was waiting inside the main door of The Inn, looking for a person that fit the description Hiram gave her. She kept waiting. Finally a man with those characteristics started walking toward the entrance. As Brice was coming into the main door of The Inn, Anna was coming out. She acted as though she was dancing inside herself when she bumped into Brice. She bounced down onto the walkway; she shook her head staring up at Brice. Brice reached down to help her. He looked like an astonished college kid. Her skirt was past her thighs and her figure was more than bewitching. "Here, take my hand," Brice said.

Anna got back on her feet. Brushed her skirt. "I've just finished an interview with the manager of the kitchen here in the hotel," she said. "The position came up only a day ago, and I really wanted it. I love this place. The manager asked several questions. I talked on what highlights my talent, and what joys I found in doing things I loved. She was moved, and smiled. And then she offered me the job. I actually hugged her. As I was coming out of the hotel door I was dancing with energy. While I was thinking about my new life I . . . bumped into you. I sure hope you didn't have any coffee in your hand."

Brice half-smiled. "I had no coffee."

"I guess I got all excited because this hotel is not just fascinating but it keeps attracting a quality crowd of campers." Anna giggled. "I mean it, the Beatles stayed here, Led Zeppelin, and David Bowie. But not just stars, classy clients stay here. There are parties, weddings, banquets, company meetings, and get this, lectures on creativity every week. This place is fantastic to work in. I'm going to work here forever."

"Nice bumping into you young lady." Brice gave a confident look. "What's your name?"

"Anna Tyers."

"Nice name." Brice continued walking forward to the large front doors of The Inn. As he walked he turned his head around toward the attractive lady.

Brice was escorted into Gage's office. "Good to see you Brice. I think you'll enjoy this." Gage brought out a large drawing of The Inn, and sat down with Brice next to the French windows. "The highlighted dots are the places we would construct Leschi's statues. You can see that they'll be built in areas so that a wide range of people can observe them. Not just guests here, but many Seattleites driving to and from work, as well as employees working in Belltown, Pioneer Square, and Chinatown. You'll get a ton of publicity. Plus there will be lighted signs around them commenting on the beauty of who Leschi was and did for this territory."

"It's a good idea. No, it's a great idea. I'll use it. But remember what I've said, I'm taking over your hotel. If you don't pass The Inn over to me, I'll bomb the fucking place."

"That's great. Do I get anything in return? How much money are you going to pay me?"

"Pay you? Are you a loose screw?"

"Brice we've hit this roulette wheel a thousand times. You can't blow this building apart, not with all the devices and cameras we have now installed. You'll also be jailed. I say, let's get Leschi exonerated. Come on Brice, let's go for it. A whole new world of possibilities and opportunities can become available."

"McClure, you do have spit and spite. But stop your shenanigans, and hand over your hotel. I'll give it back to you after I've finished my goals!" Brice got up from the chair. "I almost ruined your place last time, but next time, I'll demolish it if you just procrastinate. Will you change ownership, now!"

"Brice, this is no way to act."

Brice walked out of the room, went down the stairs, and out of the hotel. He got in his car and drove away. Unbeknownst to Brice, a car from the hotel parking lot, was following him.

"This is insane," Gage blurted out. He was in his office with Hiram. "Dillon yesterday, and Brice today, again and again. Brice declined my plan, got out of his chair, and yelled that we have to throw in the sponge and hand The Inn over to him. He slammed the door as he left." Gage kicked his left leg. "As the lady reporter said, the City of Seattle is getting very fearful of our property. They might kick us off the waterfront, if this continues."

"Easy, leg man. Ain't nothing in this world stays solid and secure. Ya gotta realize that, and not get upset by it. No matter how hard you try or how wild you resist that fact, it is a fact! But, you can learn to relax and flow. Do this and you'll find wild possibilities everywhere. Right now, I want you to look out toward the bay, and take five deep breaths. Deep breaths. OK, start. But, damn the Gods, go slowly."

Gage bit his lip, pouted, then turned toward the bay and breathed slowly. At the end of the fifth breath he turned back to Hiram. "So, big Buddha, what do we do now?"

"Dillon's going to try and be linked to Brice. And Brice is going to whack our place wild if we don't hand over ownership. But we sure ain't going to hand it over to him. So I'll call Tony D, and have him send over an expert in detection for anything on the water or in the water. We also have the beginning of some lead to where Brice's home is. Dear Anna has slyly followed Brice to his car. She took down his license plate number."

Gage almost looked amused.

CHAPTER 27

Dillon was listening to one of his security men who had been trying to find out the person behind the explosions at Gage's hotel.
"Mr. Russell we followed your suggestion and the three of us did
a round the clock surveillance of that hotel. We paid attention to
the four main people you suggested from the pictures you gave
us. The two guys, and the two gals. In the afternoon, the youngest
girl, the one called Anna, was waiting for nearly an hour just inside
the hotel's main door. She obviously was getting a little impatient.
When a particular man started coming into the hotel, she came out
the door and purposely bumped into him. She fell down. The man
helped her up. They talked. The man went into the hotel. Anna went
around the corner of the hotel and hid behind some of the ever-
greens, and . . . just waited and waited till that man came out and
went to his car. Then she copied down his license plate number. We
don't know if this man is who you're after, but for the short surveillance we've done this was the first person that seemed to have some
loose connection to the hotel, or why would she be so eagle-eyed
on this man. We followed him. This is where he lives: in Phinney
Ridge."

The security man gave Dillon the slip of paper.

"Interesting. Life's certainly a fancy casino with a deck of cards.
OK, I'm under the gun, I need to find the bomb guy. Let's see if this

is who he is, if not, we go back to the surveillance game. Get some shut-eye, and in the morning we're all off to Phinney Ridge."

Brice was at his home in Phinney Ridge in Seattle. It was around midnight. He was sipping coffee as he looked at the map of Seattle's waterfront. What would cause the Seattle government to wake up and get real? What would cause the Washington State government to get real and realize this city's name came from an Indian Chief smitten with excessive pride and insecurities? Once the white skins came to our land, Chief Seattle's primary goal was only to win favor from the white leaders. While Chief Leschi was mainly interested in maintaining respect and a flourishing future for his own people.

Could Brice really blast the whole waterfront apart? Or could he just destroy a few primary piers, then contact the government, and tell them what he was after? Anyone who had heart for this land had to truly get the government to open their eyes and see what they've been refusing to see: Chief Leschi was killed under false facts. Decade after decade this state government allowed this adversity to continue.

Politicians! They use money and grit to get elected. And, they all have a common trait: the need for approval masked with precious words and polished anger.

Brice sipped some more coffee.

Maybe . . . maybe . . . he should meet with Gage's contact at the Nisqually Indian Administration; skip the bombs and fireworks, and plead with the man to make efforts to exonerate Leschi, now. To not put it off as this state's administration was always doing.

Brice hit the table. No! He couldn't rely on that administration. He had to make inroads himself. He had to get Leschi exonerated. Brice's blood came from the Nisqually. No one was fixing these facts of history. No one was dedicating their life for a new life of liberty to be given to Chief Leschi's name.

Brice grabbed the map and looked at Pier 67, the pier that was Gage's hotel at the moment. It would be a prime target to destroy. It was the only hotel on the waterfront, a classic. People would talk for ages about its disaster. But damn it, if he did bomb it Gage wouldn't be able to get all the guests out of the building in time. And the Washington State government would never deal with him if so many people were killed. Brice kicked the table, then straightened out the paper map so he could look past the hotel's pier. There, Pier 52, the ferry terminal. Again, too many people would be killed with the explosions. It would be desirable but too detrimental.

He shook his head and looked some more at the map. Hey, what about Pier 59, the Seattle Aquarium? It was popular and held Seattle's interest. He'd hit it with explosives at night when people weren't around. Brice ardently kept looking at the map. And what about the Washington State Convention Trade Center? He could also explode it nighttime. Of course it wasn't on the water but it was close enough, and it was a prime location. These two spots could be cracked to pieces because of the government's long time ignorance to Leschi. He'd explain all this to the state government, and tell them he'd stop everything, if they'd actually legislate and—finally—exonerate Leschi; finally call forth some honor that had been lost for decades. Brice got up and slowly went to bed with a smile.

Late in the afternoon Dillon pulled onto the driveway of Brice's place, followed by two guards in another car. Dillon got out, walked over to the other car, and talked to the driver. "While I start having a conversation with this man, I want you to go into the garage and see if you can notice anything connected to bombs: activators, fuses, containers, power sources. Or even some common, small explosives, like a pipe bomb."

Dillon went up to the door and rang the doorbell twice. Brice opened the door and looked a couple times at the slick BMW. Dillon handed him a photograph of The Inn at the Pier.

Brice squinted his eyes, looked up at the man, then back down at the photograph. "There's a reason you're here?"

"I'm interested if you know of this place."

"Are you marketing something, goin' door to door?"

Dillon smiled. "No. But I know you were at this hotel yesterday. May I step in for a moment?"

"We can do the talking right here."

"Sure. My name is Dillon Russell. What's yours?"

"I don't give that information to strangers."

This man was a riot. Dillon pointed to the picture. "This hotel was battered a couple days ago by some bombshells. The guests were scared as hell. Things have settled down, but the blasts are still a talk of the town. I am not a damn cop, I just want to find the person who did that."

"Why?"

"I want to get in cahoots with him."

"This is crazy. I don't have the time to spend talking." Brice turned and started to go inside.

"A lady called Anna Tyers seemed intrigued by you," Dillon said.

Brice stopped, turned around, and scowled.

"Don't know why she was," Dillon said. "Maybe it was your looks, or it could have been something to do with your past actions to destabilize that waterfront hotel."

"Dillon," the security guy called out as he came running toward the front door. "Take a look." The man threw down some blasting caps, a couple bottles of mercury fulminate, some TNT, a few C-4s, and two rusty-looking pipe bombs.

"Well, Mr. whatever-your-name-is, it seems like you have an interest in blast and burst hardware."

"And your interest in this, is . . . what?"

"To see if you're the guy I want to ask questions to. I want to meet the man that made madness in that hotel. Are you the right person I'm after?"

"If you're not a cop. Who the hell are you? Why are you so diligent in trying to track down that man? What's going on, Dillon Russell?"

"Maybe I'm a bit like you. I'm a little reluctant to completely open up. I don't want to pass on disquieting information to some normal pancake guy. I need to find the man that has the will and wit to explode piers and people's fears. Can we go inside?"

"My God, you speak like that big man at the hotel. Look, I've got to get inside and work. Just leave." Brice shut the door.

The security man looked at Dillon.

Dillon shook his head. "The whole time he was talking I kept looking straight across to the wall. There were six photographs of Indians by rushing rivers, on horses, and sitting by glowing camp-fires. In the middle of it all there was a portrait of an Indian who looked like he was contemplating an algebra problem or something mystical. This bomb boy seems to have a great affection for them. And, given the color of his skin, he's probably Indian too." Dillon smiled and looked around the yard. "OK, we won't barge in right now. Let me do some fact-finding first. But I want the two of you to move off the driveway and position your car down the street. When that ornery fellow drives out of his driveway, I need the two of you to go around the back, and skillfully open up a window with the tools you brought along. Look for information about him anywhere in the house, especially in his office and in any files. When you've got some good info leave and get hold of me." Dillon walked to his car.

Brice spit into the kitchen sink and then went over to the desk in the main room. Were those men sent by Gage McClure to scare the hell out of him? No one knew about his motives except for Gage and Mark Schmit. He sucked down some more beer. Mark would never tell anyone about him. But Gage might hire someone like Dillon to try and work with him, so Gage would know if and when the hotel was going to be hit again. OK, OK, forget all the subplots. This evening he would collect the added cash he needed to start his efforts to demolish the two areas he had chosen. He went back to finish the details.

Later that night Brice got in his car and drove off to get the extra cash. When Dillon's two men saw the car leave, they slowly drove to Brice's home, got out, and went to the back of the house with their flashlights. There were no other houses surrounding the backyard. They walked through a small garden and came to the first of three back windows. It was a sliding window. One of the men worked a thin hacksaw blade into the window near the window's latch. When it reached the latch he pushed the hacksaw blade till the latch opened. They stepped in quietly.

The house had one large room downstairs. It was clustered with bags of paper and bunches of hardware equipment. On the far side of the room was a large sofa half covered with files and index card boxes. Next to the sofa was a small desk. It faced the wall with a painting of some tribal Indian. Under the picture was a caption in red ink: The Man. The Warrior. Our chief.

Both of Dillon's men got busy sifting through the index boxes and scattered files on the sofa. The men did quick studies of all the mess of facts and figures. "Hey, Ron, look at this." The man showed Ron a penciled headline on one of the index cards: *Gage needs to be scared out of his closed mind.* The card listed blasting equipment, time and duration of different bombs, scuba gear needed, and a divided and marked up version of Pier 67 that contained The Inn at the Pier.

They rustled through more of the loose files. "Josh, look here." The file had the name of Chief Leschi. Inside it was a picture similar to the one on the wall. "Shit, the guy we're after is a tribal daddy." They both kept looking. "Josh, more evidence." The file had papers that specified a particular boombox along with special codes for the speakers. It also contained an added factor: Place the boombox in one of the rooms on the middle floor of the hotel. "Man, we've got some key information. Let's take the files and cards, and get on back to Dillon."

It was around eight in the evening. The nightclub Brice went to was packed to the hilt. The stand-up bar was jammed elbow to elbow, and the crowd of customers were laughing and smiling throughout the large room. Waitresses, wearing sexy skirts, were twisting and turning through the pack of people. The bartender was fat and husky with short hair and a smooth face. He was lighting cigarettes and pouring drinks with the speed of a cheetah.

Brice Hafer and a large man squeezed through the crowd. Brice went to one end of the bar. The heavyweight guy went to the other end of the bar. Brice held up his hand and ordered a cold beer. As he was being served, a bomb blew up at the other end of the bar. Shock waves traveled throughout the tavern. Half the customers screamed and yelled. Many people started running. Several women tripped and crashed into the tables. Waitresses dropped trays. Brice pulled out a small pistol and slammed it into the bartender's belly. "Quickly, open both registers."

"What the—"

"You say one more word and you're dead. Now open them."

The bartender was hesitating, but another blast erupted. Everyone was startled. "Open it now."

The registers were opened, Brice took out all the bills, turned, and went out the side door. No one noticed him; they were too busy with tension and terror.

After Brice and the heavyweight guy got home, Brice called Mark Schmit. "Mark, I've finally got the extra money needed to obtain our bombs. Get over here and I'll give you all the cash so you can buy the explosives in order to rip apart those two sites in Seattle."

CHAPTER 28

The next morning Dillon gathered his needed information and drove to Brice's house. He was followed by his two security men in an F-350. Dillon got out of his car and knocked on Brice's front door. Brice's car was there, but there was no response. Dillon knocked again. Still nothing. Dillon turned and waved his hand. The security truck revved up, drove in almost warp speed, and crashed right through the door. The men got out of the van, ran over to Brice, and shoved him down on the long sofa. They pulled out their guns. Brice looked like a member of a rock band gone wild.

Dillon walked in, lit a cigarette, and strolled over to Brice. He sucked on his cigarette for a moment then handed Brice a file with Gage's name on it. "It's your file filled with a bunch of loose papers. Some of my boys broke into your house last night while you were gone, and collected this data." Dillon pulled out a sheet of paper that had a highlighted design of Pier 67, Gage's pier. "In this same file you have listed blasting equipment along with time and duration of different bombs. Brice, you're the guy that bombed Gage's pier. No question about it. I need to join up with you to blast that bastard's hotel totally apart." Dillon took another long pull on the cigarette. "Come on over to the chairs, we need to talk."

They both walked to the chairs.

"Well, Mr. Russell, you do have the balls of a corporate exec. You set a goal and reach it with the speed."

"Brice, why did you even start to think about blowing up the famous Inn at the Pier?"

"You're asking this so you can take control of Gage's hotel? What the hell is your reason?"

"Will you stop your damn questioning and simply start answering!"

Brice turned and looked at the crashed door. This Dillon character was full of drive. Hell, the guy would probably have his muscle men beat the living crap out of him if he didn't surrender any information. "Mr. Russell, I am having—like you may be having—a rough road on life. But, it's a journey I choose to be on. It's full of ambition and possibilities. If I ever want to have others join me, I'll reach out. If I don't want others to conspire with me, then I'll keep traveling the road on my own. Go on and knock the hell out of me if you wish, but you'll get no information from me. Got it? So leave."

"You idiot. I'm here to help both of us. You obviously haven't succeeded with your threats to Gage, and therefore you haven't accomplished your goal. Whatever the reason you have had for shaking up Gage's hotel, let me help you. Because I need him to know how badly his hotel could be damaged again if he doesn't deal with you, and with me. I need him to sell certain land properties to me here in Washington State, but he keeps refusing my money and my request. I need a crowbar of control, an advantage, over him. And I think you can help me, as I might be able to help you."

"Dillon, I don't want to go into our missions in life. I want you out of here and not crash-banging into my home again. I'll leave you alone; you leave me alone."

"You sound like a two year old, almost crying 'cause mommy ain't givin' out any more cookies. Only Gage knows of your attempt to blow up his prized possession. And now, I've got evidence. You'll get evicted if I turn it all in, and you'll end up doing Buck Rogers time. Hold your impulses and let's grab some brandy, go into your study, and do what's common for most yardbirds: talk on breakin' free from a tug-of-war."

"Again Mr. Russell, you're almost talking like Gage's muscle man. But you don't have the muscle." Brice got up and spit on the floor.

The security man dashed over, pounded him back onto the sofa, and smacked his face.

Dillon strolled into the kitchen and opened several cabinets. Found a bottle of scotch, poured two glasses, and went back and sat down next to Brice.

"You're right, we can go on and on. Or, maybe we could sip a little and just start to talk—a little." Dillon drank some scotch and handed the bottle to Brice.

Brice paused for a moment. He needed this man out of his house, out of his life. The bastard was like a haul truck with double wheels and a broken axle. Brice got up and took the bottle. He sipped some scotch and walked to a bookcase at the end of the sofa with several drawers. He opened a middle drawer. The lights were off so no one could see what he was reaching for. "Dillon, you have guts and a lot of tact. I think we can get together." He was lying like hell. "Here." Brice pulled a pin, and threw one of his custom made, low intensity, hand grenades at the two security men. Immediately Brice grabbed another and threw it at Dillon. The grenades exploded. One security guy was in a coma. The other looked scatterbrained, but functioning. Brice pushed that man onto the floor. He turned to Dillon. Dillon was in a coma. Brice went back to the man on the floor, picked him up, and lifted his gun in the air. "I want you to take these two men out of here in the push cart." Brice pointed to the cart underneath the stairs. "Take these two assholes to your truck, and get out of here."

When everyone was in the truck, the F-350 left. Brice shook his head and went back to the house. He walked over to his desk and finished the outlines for the two potential locations to be bombed. He kept studying the design of the Seattle Aquarium and the Washington State Convention and Trade Center, when there was a knock on the front door. Christ, not Dillon again. He punched the desk.

He picked up his revolver and opened the door. Gage and Anna were staring at him. "My God," Brice said. "First the Dillon character shows up here about an hour ago. The man who wants to blast your hotel to pieces because you ain't anteing up some land you have. And now you Gage, you come to my house. How did the two of you ever find out where I live? You're sharp McClure. Are you here to tell me you found a way to exonerate Leschi? Or, are you here to see if I want to hire your new employee?" Brice pointed at Anna. "She's cute, but I've got no coffee shop in my house that needs an assistant."

"What! Dillon was over here?" Gage said. "And yes, he's pretty upset because I won't cower to his wishes. But I'll deal with him later. Right now, I want to try and get us to pull together on two points. To find some unity. You have your dreams. I've got mine. We can honor each of them."

"Mr. McClure, I slammed and slashed our last conversation because of your insistence to have me move in your direction. You can't keep tossing your can of worms in front of me. You can't even—"

Anna interrupted and moved closer to Brice. "You know I love The Inn. It can't get hurt by this Dillon idiot, or even by you. Mr. McClure has told me about your wish to free Chief Leschi's name and history. He can work with you on it. I can work with you on it. Hell, the whole hotel can work on it. Could we try and work together?"

"You're sweet young lady, but Gage is not so open-minded. He's got the clamps of a capitalist no matter how he talks."

"What makes you think that?" she said.

"Did you not even hear him? He keeps insisting that I have to obey his thoughts, his wishes. Those are not soft suggestions, they're pure capitalistic commands. His wants are to be observed and obeyed. I would have—"

"Dammit Brice, would you listen?" Gage said. "The Inn is ranked number one in Seattle, or was ranked number one. Because of your darn bomb explosions last week, we've dropped far below the top spot. All I was doing—"

"We were able to set off those bombs because you can't stop us anymore. You understand that? We're using devices that make the sound waves your underwater detectors send out invisible to detect. Now listen up, and then shut up, I'm taking over your hotel. I've decided I'm not going to bomb the hotel to hell; I'm going to use it for a different reason. But I will keep up my irritating blasts that will destroy your reputation and have no more guests wanting to stay at your digs. Then you'll need to surrender your hotel to me, or keep getting more and more hurt by the press."

Gage looked at Anna, then back at Brice. "Brice, maybe you need—"

"McClure, turn around and leave! And, if you attempt to come back, or try to corral me in any way, I'll kill you with technology." Brice pointed to his ceiling. It had half a dozen pointed tubes scattered throughout the ceiling. "Those are TR devices that discharge ricin mist and cause death within hours. After we leave each other, I'll have them activated. Goodbye."

Brice closed the front door.

CHAPTER 29

When Dillon was delivered to his house and woke up from his blasted coma he took a hot shower. He thought about his whole damned situation. He dried off and got dressed. Then he poured himself some coffee and got on the phone. "Jess, get over here with your two men."

When the gang arrived, Dillon turned to the Jess. "Jess, get the video camera ready. While you're doing that I'll talk to your muscle men."

In about 20 minutes, everyone entered the second bedroom. Cindy was tied up on the bed, wiggling intensely while she looked at the group of guys.

The two muscle men started walking to the bed. Cindy cried out, yelling and screaming. They untied her.

"Please stop this. You can't do this!" Cindy's face was as red as blood. Her voice was tangled with fears and tears.

She was stripped naked, slapped several times on her ass, and turned over several times. All this was recorded on video, including her howling and screaming.

The video, along with a video player, was delivered to Matt Hastings at his farm. The men had barged into the house and threw the video disk on the floor. "Look at the video you bastard. It's your wife on film. You need to have Gage give your land to Dillon. You don't make this happen, and your wife will be driven to hell, slowly and painfully." They turned and went out the door.

Matt felt like a black cloud in the middle of a white sky. He picked up the disk and inserted it into the video player, and watched the horror. How could he have let this happen? He didn't protect Cindy. He isn't protecting the farm. Everything will be all gone. She'll be dead, lifeless. He'd be lifeless. He couldn't continue on without the ways she hugged him and helped him.

He had to save her. He had to father his sons into bright boys, and fun farmers. And without Cindy, he couldn't do it. Without Cindy, this life would be a road of regret.

Matt went out and looked at the barn he had reconstructed along with his sons. He turned and gazed toward the fields of his farm; he kept looking at the crops and vegetables that not only earned him money, but fed his family with emotion and food, and with love. He needed to get out of this double trouble. He needed Gage McClure. Matt went into the house and made the call.

Gage answered. "Matt?"

"Gage, I'm in a quicksand of chaos. Dillon's men just left. They dropped off a video of Cindy being molested by his men. She was yelling and crying. They said she'll be sexed and slammed to death if you don't give Dillon my farm. This can't happen to her! It can't happen to the farm. Gage, you're no saint, but I beg you: please find a way to rescue her."

"Matt, in my handbook on life, friendship, within and without, is the number one key to this life. I'm with Anna right now, driving back to The Inn. Why don't you and the boys jump in the car and come on over to the hotel. Friendship, my man. We'll find a way to move through this and get Cindy back. It can happen, and, damn it, it will happen."

"Gage, I can't hurt the boys. I am stressed and anxious. It wouldn't be safe for me to drive."

"OK, OK, try and keep calm. I'll have one of my seaplanes jet on over to Cle Elum lake and pick you and the boys up. The pilot will call you as he's getting close. He'll fly you back to The Inn. I'll be waiting for you."

Anna and Gage got back to The Inn and hustled upstairs to talk to Hiram. He took the two of them out to his private sundeck and listened to Gage.

"Well, it seems you had a pretty testy conversation with Brice," Hiram said.

Gage nodded. "Obviously, the guy's inflexible. He's going to hurt The Inn, as well as other spots on the waterfront. And then, to really make things wild, Matt called as we were in the car."

Anna burst into the conversation. "Dillon has not only captured Matt's wife, but now he's taking aggressive steps to have us give Matt's farm to him. He forced Matt to look at a video of Cindy being sexually abused."

"Hiram," Gage said. "I've one of our seaplanes fly over to Matt's place, pick him up, and his sons, and fly them back here." Gage shook his head, hit his chest, and began to shed a tear. "I keep trying to protect him, and I keep losing out."

"Gage, slow down. I've told ya this a million times: When I'm shocked, or you're shocked, we normally tend to breath in quick, short breaths from the chest. However, when we can focus on breathing in and out slowly, we're able to change our fuckin' inside traffic jams, and those ugly thoughts begin to back off. Do some deep breathing for a minute."

Gage listened to his big dog. He closed his eyes and took in several deep breaths, again and again. Then he opened his eyes and looked at Hiram. "It does lessen some of the upstairs howls. But I'm still pressured in the heart. I don't know what to do to save Cindy. Cindy and Matt need each other. They have fire for each other, and they have a trust that glues their connection tight."

161

"Well, the cornerstone to getting Cindy back is to locate Dillon, and then do some high-pounding negotiating."

"We've tried like hell to find him. We can't."

"Ever hear of a group called Paper Lace? Them boys sing a phrase called, 'give em more than they can take.' Why don't we have someone—one of Tony's men—drop off a pile of cash to one of Dillon Russell's land managers? He'll tell the manager his company wants to buy one of Dillon's cherished farms. His company knows Dillon is a hard bargainer, so they're offering one million—up front. Tony's guy will say: 'I've got the cash right here. No matter how negotiations turn out, your Dillon keeps the cash.' "

"What!" Gage yelled out. "Where the hell do we get that kind of money?"

"Don't worry about that just yet. Main thing is to have Tony's second man wait outside in the background when the bag of cash is being delivered to the land manager. Tony's man will keep waiting till a car pulls up and someone gets out and walks up to the land manager's office. When this person walks back to his car with the bag of cash, Tony's man will follow where the cash-man goes. Most likely it'll be where Dillon hangs out. Or, at least we'll have an idea of someone who is in direct contact with Dillon, and we can shadow that new guy till he leads us to Dillon."

"You do have grit. And a bunch of brains. But now, what the hell do we do to save the hotel from Brice's obsession to take it over, or abolish it with bombs?" Gage stuffed his hands into his pockets. He had to protect his pier and his people. How the hell do you stop a maniac like this? How—

"Ease up, good buddy. We've handled fury before, and we've always won out. We'll tackle Dillon. And, we'll deal with Brice. Just be sure ya keep focusin' in on the truth: when you change your thoughts, you change your life. Keep a smile swinging on your face, and inside your heart. Let's go."

CHAPTER 30

A well dressed man walked into a small building of a land management company in Rosalia, Washington. "I'd like to speak to the manager, Lucas Beckett. I'm Paul Jennings from the Dixon Group, in Helena, Montana."

"What would you like to talk to Mr. Beckett about?" the receptionist answered.

"We're interested in buying some farmland your company owns. It's a cherished property so we thought hard on how to introduce our interest. I've got an unusual offer for Mr. Beckett. May I see him?"

The receptionist excused herself. Several minutes later she escorted Paul Jennings into Mr. Beckett's office. Mr. Beckett motioned to the chair in front of his desk. "Mr. Jennings, we don't sell any of the properties we have acquired. Mr. Russell, our owner, makes that very clear. All our farm lands are teamed together to give us an unusual high profit, unique in this industry. We sell none of our land to no one."

"I definitely understand. But I am willing to go way past a formal approach of acquisition." Paul lifted his leather bag onto Mr. Beckett's desk, opened it, and spilled some loose money out of the bag. "Mr. Beckett, there is one million dollars right here. This will be a down deposit on our proposal to Mr. Russell. If he does not accept our proposal, this deposit will not be returned. It will be Mr. Russell's forever."

"What the hell are you doing! Are you some thug who wants to acquire enough land to traffic illegal farm products? I think you should leave."

"Mr. Beckett, I'm not interested in anything illegal. All I wish to do is to have Mr. Russell listen to our intentions, our plans and purposes of increasing our harvest of cotton so a subsidiary of ours can make a new brand of jeans. We also want to increase our interest in bioplastics from sugarcane, wheat, and corn. All my company wants is to widen its market—as, I'm sure your corporation does. Maybe we can't make a deal, or maybe we can. But at least can we have a meeting and decide?"

"I said, you should leave. You are not—"

Paul slapped the desk. "Of course we can go round and round. Of course, you think I'm a nothing. But will you please—" Paul scooped up the money, and put it back into the bag. Then handed the bag to Mr. Beckett. "Will you please honor my only wish: to meet Mr. Russell so I can make my request clear. Would you just do that one thing? If we met and Mr. Russell refuses, this money is his."

Mr. Beckett closed one eye.

"May we meet tomorrow at noon?"

Mr. Beckett cracked half a smile. "Well, this is slightly unusual. But you do have audacity and drive. I suppose we can all meet."

"Thank you, I'll see both of you tomorrow." Paul Jennings walked out of the corner office building and into his car. He drove onto Josephine Avenue. On the other side of Josephine was a blue Ford Mustang with a quiet man in the driver's seat. Paul nodded and drove past the Mustang.

About an hour later a company car drove onto the driveway of the land management building. A man got out and walked into the small building. In less than thirty minutes the man came out with the same bag that Paul Jennings had given to Mr. Beckett. The company car backed out of the drive, and onto Josephine Avenue. The Ford Mustang followed the company car. After a forty minute drive the company car pulled into a driveway near Liberty Lake close to Spokane. The driver got out of the car and walked toward the house. The front door opened. He went in. The Ford Mustang waited a moment, then drove down the street.

It was six in the evening and one of The Inn's seaplanes was landing close to the hotel's pier. It taxied to the east side of the pier where Gage was waiting. After it docked, the pilot hit the switch so Gage could open the plane's door. Matt and his children came out of the plane.

Matt looked at Gage. "It was a beautiful flight, filled with great sights of water and mountains. And now, here, at your place: fantastic waters, and more remarkable, majestic mountains. But the boys were quiet and somber through most of the ride. They want their mom. They cry at night, missing her soft kisses, hugs and warmth. Gage, I do the same damn thing. It's not just that I miss her; I need her. I can't live without her." Matt crashed into Gage and hugged him as he swept away some tears.

"Matt, we've already taken action. We're making inroads as to where Dillon is. When we get the location, Hiram will take his back-up boys and coral Dillon, and rescue Cindy. We're going to bring her back to you. We're going to do this Matt."

"Gage, maybe I should just give up my farm. Give it to Dillon, and get Cindy back." More tears.

"There is no way you're going to give up your gold and toss away your passion. You need your farm, your land, and your lady. You're going to keep all of it. Come on, let's get your boys up to The Inn. They need sleep and some cozy comfort." Gage gave the kids a couple big hugs, and tousled their hair. Then he grabbed Matt by the shoulders and gave him a firm hug. "Matt, Cindy is going to come back. The ball's rollin', and it won't stop till she's on your range ridin' broncos with the rest of you."

CHAPTER 31

Brice knew the Seattle Aquarium and the Convention Center had to be exploded at night to give him hard leverage to have the stupid state government open their eyes for once, and see that the verdict to hang Chief Leschi was totally unwise and unfair. Leschi needed to be exonerated NOW, not in another ten years.

Pier 59, which housed the aquarium, would be blown apart with TNT and RDX that would be delivered underwater. It would be a Ferris wheel of fire, then sink to the bottom of the bay. His main technician and a crew of six would organize everything. They would work from midnight to three in the morning installing the explosives. All the work would be done out of sight, in the water, and under the pier.

Brice sucked down more scotch, with confidence.

All of a sudden, there was some pounding on top of the roof. Brice spit out the scotch and looked up. More pounding.

"Brice, this is Anna up here on your roof. I wanna come in. But, if it's on, will you turn off the damn poison gas and powder. I need to talk to you. I'll come down and come to the front door. I've got something for you."

Brice opened the door. Anna was wearing no clothes. She was completely naked.

Brice's mouth almost dropped to the ground. He lost all of his anger.

Anna leaned forward and gave Brice a hug. "Would you get a blanket for me. I need some warmth." She squeezed him hard again. Her breasts flattened out over his chest.

Brice was red in the face as he left her standing and went to the other room for a blanket. He came back and wrapped her in the blanket. "What . . . what are you doing here?"

"Brice, can we go to your office and sit down?"

They both sat down in his office. "Brice, I know I shocked your insides. And you probably might even think I'm a little insane. Actually, my life has been pretty twisted. I had foul parents and I lived on the streets for years. I was nothin' but a runaway. I was beaten up and fucked many times while I lived on the streets. Alone and lost. I never knew who I was, until I met Gage McClure. He's helped straighten me out. And I owe him a lot, but it's a long road to win yourself back from the black mud of nightmares."

Brice closed one eye. His youth was similar. He grew up in a one room shack in Tacoma's East Side. Not a slum area, but it was damn dangerous. Tacoma had street gangs that picked on any non-whites with insults and name-calling. He got slapped around and hit many times for not just being an Indian, but a Nisqually. Brice fought back with slander and spit, but was always overpowered. He hated it. He hated thinking about it now. Why was she even mentioning all this? "Anna, you're an upfront girl, but I don't see why you're here?"

"I'm here to finally give you a piece of good news. Gage didn't think you'd let him in to tell you it all. So, I volunteered to make your night sparkle." She tugged at her blanket. "Bert Collin, head of the Nisqually Indian Administration, says that he has finally won victory: both houses of the state legislature are in the process of passing resolutions stating that Leschi was wrongly convicted and executed. They have already asked the state supreme court to cancel Leschi's conviction." She rubbed his hand.

Brice looked into her eyes, then up to the ceiling, and then back down to Anna again, and gave her a kiss. "This is outrageous. I can't believe it. How . . . when was the victory?"

"I have no idea, but Gage has the information. Let's jump into your car and crash on over to The Inn?" She tightened the blanket and got up. "Come on, big-daddy. Let's go."

Brice's car turned off of Alaskan Way and onto the driveway at The Inn. Anna and Brice got out of the car and walked to the main entrance. Anna took Brice's car keys and handed it to the doorman. "Park the car and return the key to Gage's box."

They walked into the lobby. Several guests stared at an almost naked girl with only a blanket wrapped around her. The front desk lady cried out, "Anna, Anna, you're back, you're safe."

Anna and Brice walked into her office. She called Gage. "Gage, we're here. I've got Brice in my office. He needs an explanation as to what's going on, what's happening. Do you want us to come up to you, or do you want to grab a coffee in my office?"

"Let's have a meeting up here."

When the two of them came in, Gage's eyes burst open. "Anna . . . you've got no clothes on. Just a—"

"It's Martha Stewart's new design. Come on, let's start spilling the beans for Brice."

Gage poured some drinks, and they all walked to the alcove by the windows overlooking the bay. Gage turned to Brice and sat down. "Well, it looks like your hero, Chief Leschi, is finally going to be admired and honored by a government that put him to death ages ago. A Washington Historical Court of Justice has just been set up yesterday after the State Legislature passed a resolution urging action to right a gross injustice. It is going to hold a formal hearing at Tacoma's Washington State Historical Museum, Dec. 10. Seven judges from the state's courts and a tribal judge will hear testimony from four lawyers and eleven witnesses with a genuine understanding of what took place."

Brice stopped sipping his brandy.

"Some of the witnesses will be Nisqually tribal members, lawyers, and legislators. Senator Daisy Cabtel will also be there. She's already said to the press that rather than asking for a pardon from the governor, she's going to ask the state Supreme Court to overturn the conviction of Chief Leschi upheld by the Supreme Court of the Territory of Washington in December 1857. This way, Leschi will be exonerated, not simply excused for any killing." Gage winked. "Daisy's not only sexy, but she's got a sharp mind, too. She said in the press interview that asking for a pardon would be easier but it'd be an incomplete victory for Leschi." Gage shot his hand out toward the bay. "Brice, you got some knife-edged people pullin' for your Leschi's liberation."

"McClure, how the hell has this happened? I've been trying for a year to push government assholes to my cause. But no results. Have you maneuvered all this? Are you doing this so you can manipulate me or other people now and later down the road?"

"No way, Brice. And yes, even though your actions have been pretty reckless at times, I do believe in your cause. I've told you this before."

Brice looked straight into Gage's eyes.

"The main man behind all of this Brice, is Bert Collin. You keep telling me that you know him. But you don't want to meet him. He's been pushing and propelling the need to reestablish Chief Leschi's name and honor before you even jumped onto the market game. He's united all the Nisqually and circled them into a ramrod of political propulsion. And they finally have won leverage. As I said, the Historical Court has been formed and ready to litigate on a new ruling for Chief Leschi. It looks like it's a go."

Brice got out of his chair, lifted Gage up, squeezed his shoulders, and then turned him toward the picture windows. "I am sorry McClure for the difficulty I've given you. And, I thank you like a wet-eyed cougar for helping. You're one goddamn good man." Brice waved his hand out toward the bay. "And you've got a remarkable hotel, based on passion and a predilection for sharp creativity."

Anna jumped up, dropped her blanket to the floor, and with a nude body, bear-hugged her boss.

CHAPTER 32

Hiram and a couple of Tony's crew had flown to Spokane. They were now driving to a house in the city of Liberty Lake. It was the small house that had been put under surveillance by Tony D several days ago. Hiram stopped the van and had two of Tony's guys go into the garage and check the license plate. Yup, it was Dillon's car.

All of Tony's men put on a pair of boxing gloves and walked to the front window. They shattered the window and went in. Some of them stayed by the window, the others ran upstairs to the second floor; but bullets started firing in the dark. They crashed into the nearest room and got out their guns.

"Get the hell out of here," Dillon yelled. "I've called the cops. They're on the way. You idiots are going to be cuffed if you don't run out of—"

Dillon was hit in the back with a bat. He fell to the floor. The other man hit Dillon with his boxing glove and knocked him out. The men took Dillon out to the car and sped off to a cottage on the other side of the lake.

When Dillon woke up from his stupor, Hiram handed him a cup of coffee. "Well Dillon, you're a hard guy to handle at times, but a wealthy one. And, you just received some big bucks for free. It all came from some contact Gage knows. It didn't come from some businessman who wants to buy one of your properties."

"What? That scam was your doing?"

"It takes wit and wisdom to deal with you. Like I've said, you're a crafty man. You can scare the hell out of some people, as you've done with Matt. He needs his wife back. And he sure ain't keen on you trying to take his farm. So we thought a big bundle of hay might be a pretty neat way to find you."

"So, what do you want from me? What do I have to do so you won't do your little boy thing, and get all mad, and out of control?"

"Charming, Dillon. What I want is to know where Cindy is? And then have you go with us to get her. Now, before you yell back. Let me give you something." Hiram hit Dillon in the face, then tore off part of his shirt, and drew out a knife. "You make any more round-abouts and I won't kill you, I'll just slice open your fuck'n chest and let blood flow out of you, along with parts of your fuck'n heart and lungs. Which is it Dillon? Help us out, or fume in the fires of hell?"

"You lousy bastard. You rely on your might more than your brains. You force people to bend to your appetite and attitudes. You don't give them any options. You're like a bad-ass husband to his wife." Dillon spit on the floor.

"Ain't sayin' you're wrong or right. But I am divin' into your chest." Hiram ripped open Dillon's shirt some more and lifted the knife up to Dillon's face."

"WAIT," Dillon cried out. "WAIT. Stop this."

"Where's Cindy? Tells us now, or you're toast."

"She's upstairs locked in one of the bedrooms in my mansion over in Spokane."

"Interesting. The girl's stuffed in a beautiful mansion, and you've stuffed yourself inside this small sawdust box. Come on, get up. We're headin' to Spokane."

Hiram was in the front seat of the van. Tony's men and Dillon were in the back seat. When they arrived at the mansion, Dillon opened his private gates. The waterfall ponds guided them through the estate to the mansion's front door. A stately butler opened the door and escorted them all into the foyer. Then—a team of Dillon's guards pointed guns at everyone.

Dillon shouted out, "Hiram, if you or any of your men start to pull your forty-fives, you'll all be shot in seconds." He turned to the butler. "Carl, check—"

Hiram rammed into the lead gunman. At the same time, one of Tony's men fell on the floor, moaning like a whale. Two of the gunmen abruptly looked down at the moaning man. While they were looking, Tony's other man shot both of them. Hiram picked the lead gunman up and pushed him over to his two wounded cohorts, then shoved Dillon against the wall. "Dillon, you run on fears that blind your damn reality." Hiram punched a gun onto Dillon's chest. "OK, take me to Cindy, now."

Hiram followed Dillon to a bedroom on the third floor. Dillon unlocked the door and they both walked in.

Cindy quickly turned around. She was sitting on a bed next to an aquarium. Her mouth was wide open, her eyes were wet, and her face was tight. She looked like a ballet dancer that had just lost her balance on stage.

"Cindy, don't worry. I'm Hiram Smith. I'm going to take you home, back to Matt and your children. They want you; they love you; good lord, they need you. Come on, let's get out of this hell house."

They left Dillon at his mansion, drove to the Spokane airport, and flew back to Seattle. Two of The Inn's cars were waiting for them at the airport. Tony's men got in one of the cars. Cindy and Hiram entered the other car. Off they went to the hotel.

Gage, Matt, and the boys were waiting just outside the lobby by a small waterfall with lights and color.

"Mommy." Her sons came running toward the car. "Mommy. Mommy." Cindy opened the door. Her boys banged into the back seat, kissing and hugging Cindy all over her face. She hugged them back fiercely from their heads to their hearts.

Matt stood still laughing and crying, while holding Gage's hand with a tight grip. "Thank you Gage for all your–" His words were slipping out of his mouth like some soft ice cream. Matt wiped his mouth, gave Gage a friend-to-friend punch, and then ran to Cindy.

"Everyone," Gage said, "we're going to take you up to a private suite so you can kiss each other for a year." Hiram and Gage escorted the family into the hotel and up to a top floor suite overlooking the bay. Gage gave a hug to Cindy. "We'll meet you all for a beautiful breakfast tomorrow morning."

Hiram and Gage left the room. As they walked down the hall, they looked like two giant pandas with wide and warm eyes. "Well, we did it Gage. We took on two bundles of burden, filled with threats and thunder, and came out ahead of the game. Individually, they almost ruined you. Collectively, they were blackjacking The Inn, and causing wild alarm to our guests. But once again, our tenacity and talent set us free. Gage, you're one hell of a big gun that shines through this hotel. Hell, you are the hotel."

Gage smiled, grabbed Hiram, and smacked him on the cheek with a kiss.

Hiram shoved him away. "Damn you, Gage. You do anymore of your kissin' shit, and I'll toss you in the goddamn bay with a bomb on your back." Hiram looked at his watch. "I'm starved. Let's have Charlie cook up something special for us." Hiram slapped his good buddy on the shoulder. "Let's go, amigo."

ABOUT THE AUTHOR

TC WALTERS grew up in the Northeast and eventually relocated to Seattle in the Pacific Northwest. He started his career as a young limousine driver. Soon he purchased his own limousine, and with it he went from one Seattle hotel to another promoting his service. He met many exceptional people and traveled to many interesting places around Seattle and in Canada. Several months later, he actually had a dream of not only making people laugh, but helping them become clever and creative. So, he started his second career as a small town actor. His company was called the Fantasy Merchants. He had himself and his staff dress up in outrageous costumes and crash into different company meeting rooms. The fact was, the Fantasy Merchants were hired to not only interrupt a business meeting—but—cause the astonished people to laugh a little, and open up their creativity and imagination. This venture evolved into the beginning of a creative lecturing service for a host of businesses. While this phase of his career was going forward, he began writing essays. Ultimately, he went further and started writing his first book, *The Ancient Burden of Fear*, along with his second novel, *The Ancient Burden of Misery*.

www.ingramcontent.com/pod-product-compliance
Lightning Source LLC
Chambersburg PA
CBHW022118170626

46808CB00002B/762